A Totally 80s Christmas

A Holiday Novella

Totally 80s Mysteries
Book 4

Books by D.A. Wilkerson

Totally 80s Mysteries

A Totally Killer Wedding
Most Likely to Kill
Of Heist and Men
A Totally 80s Christmas

Mystery Journals

Mysterious Musings
My Totally Suspect Notebook

A Totally 80s Christmas

D.A. Wilkerson
Mystery Author
danawilkerson.com

A Totally 80s Christmas
Totally 80s Mysteries Book 4
by D.A. Wilkerson

© 2022 Dana Wilkerson

Designed in the USA
Images and fonts used under license by Canva

Published by Dana Wilkerson, LLC
Edmond, OK
danawilkerson.com

First Edition: October 2022

Paperback ISBN: 978-1-948148-36-8
eBook ISBN: 978-1-948148-37-5

Dedicated to my mom, who snuck out of work to go to the local hardware store and buy my first Cabbage Patch Kid during the 1983 Christmas CPK craze

ONE

"YOU SURE YOU DON'T want to come in?" I looked hopefully at Mitchell from where I sat plastered against his side in his pickup.

"I need to get home before the snow hits." He curled his right arm more securely around me and pressed his lips to my temple.

"You can stay here." I placed my hand on his chest. "No need to drive an hour tonight, only to turn around and drive an hour back to see me again tomorrow."

When Mitchell came to town, he often stayed overnight at the Oak Street Hotel—otherwise known as The Osh—in downtown Cherry Hill, but the hotel was booked solid for the Christmas holiday, so Mitchell had planned to head back home to Jefferson City after our date.

"Spending the night here would not be a good idea, and you know it. Don't test my resolve, Beckett Monahan. You want to take things slow for reasons that only reside in that gorgeous head of yours," he tapped my forehead, "and I'm doing my best to abide by your wishes."

I inwardly cringed at his comment about not knowing why I didn't want to rush our relationship, but I smiled and said, "You're the strongest man I know. You can handle it."

"A man has his limits. I'm not coming in."

We watched several snowflakes land on the windshield as

George Strait sang about a chair on the radio.

"You'll be fine." I pointed at the living room window, which was lit up. "Aunt Star is here to chaperone." My aunt Starla was kind enough to let me live with her when I moved back to my hometown three years earlier, and I had never gotten around to finding my own place.

A few more flakes fell, glinting in the glow of the streetlight before melting on the warm glass.

Mitchell's fingers played with one of my long, auburn curls. "Starla isn't staying over at Darren's?"

Aunt Star had been dating Cherry Hill's Deputy Chief of Police Darren Turley for almost a year, and lately she was spending more and more time at his place.

"Not tonight. His brother's family is in town for Christmas, and his teenage nephews are sleeping at his house."

Snow began falling in earnest, swirling around the truck.

"Come on," I squeezed his thigh. "You've already lost the race with the snow. There's nowhere else you need to be until Christmas Day, which is still four days away. Stay. We have a guest room, you know."

He moved my hand to my own leg. "You're going to be the death of me."

"Then you'll die happy."

He chuckled as headlights flashed through the back window and tires crunched on the gravel driveway behind us. The garage door opened, and my aunt's red Camaro Z28 pulled past us into the empty spot next to my yellow Ford Pinto.

"Hmm. That's weird," I said. "I thought she was already home. She doesn't usually leave any lights on when she's not here."

"You *should* leave a light on, so people think you're home. It helps keep burglars away," Mitchell said.

"Yes, Detective Crowe." I grinned at him. "Come on. I'm not letting you leave with it snowing like this."

"All right." Mitchell switched off the engine. "But I don't have anything to wear to church in the morning."

"What you're wearing now is fine." Some of the farmers in the congregation wore jeans to church, so he wouldn't look out of place in his Levis and black button-up shirt. "We can toss your clothes in the wash if you want."

Mitchell hopped out of the truck and gripped my waist to slide me across the seat to him. He gave me a quick kiss before setting me on my feet.

"What will I wear while my clothes are being washed?" He took my hand and led me around the front of the vehicle.

I gave him a cheeky look. "I have a lovely hot pink and orange floral robe that would look divine on you."

Mitchell's laugh was cut off by a shriek from Aunt Star, who stood in the doorway from the garage into the kitchen. He dropped my hand and raced to her. I limped along behind him, courtesy of a badly set broken leg from childhood.

He guided my stunned aunt away from the door. "Back to the truck. Both of you."

I obeyed without question, and surprisingly Aunt Star did, too. Mitchell unlocked the passenger door, flung it open, and pressed the button on the glove compartment. When he turned around, he held a handgun. I gasped, but it shouldn't have surprised me that my detective boyfriend carried a firearm in his vehicle, even when he was on vacation.

He tossed me his keys. "Get in and lock the doors," he ordered. "Don't get out until I say so."

We both nodded and climbed into the vehicle. I turned on the engine so we could stay warm, while he headed back into the house. Aunt Star locked her door and reached over to grab my hand.

"What's going on?" I asked her.

"Somebody broke into the house."

"Again?" We had a break-in back in June as well.

"What do you think is happening in there?"

"Probably nothing exciting. Mitchell and I had been sitting out here in the truck for at least ten minutes. If anybody was still inside when we pulled up, they would have seen or heard us and left a long time ago." I pointed at the front of the house. "You notice anything weird about the front window, other than the light being on when neither of us were home?"

"What?"

"No Christmas tree. We should be able to see its outline through the sheer curtains."

"How are you so calm?" My aunt was calm in most situations, but when guns were involved, she got extremely nervous, and understandably so.

I shrugged. "I guess I'm getting used to this kind of thing."

"Please don't say that."

"I wish it weren't true." Two murders and a bank robbery in our hometown of 3,224 in less than a year should have prompted me to move away. Instead, the crime spree made me fiercely protective of my little town.

I turned the radio up and switched it to a Top 40 station to distract Aunt Star. She hummed along to the end of "We Built This City" and then Hall & Oates' version of "Jingle Bell Rock." As I began to grow nervous myself, Mitchell emerged from the house, gun no longer in sight. My aunt released a long breath and let go of my hand. She unlocked her door, and Mitchell opened it.

"The house is clear. You can come in, but don't touch anything. I need you to tell me what's missing."

He helped Aunt Star out and gave her a brief hug. I climbed out behind her, and he cocooned me in his arms for a moment before leading us back into the garage. Sirens sounded in the far distance as we stepped into the kitchen.

"Frank and Jake are on their way from the station," Mitchell explained. Aunt Star and I knew Officers Frank Nichols and Jacob Park well, not only because we were both dating police officers, but also due to our involvement in solving the previous crimes. "Darren should be here soon, too."

Glass covered the kitchen floor from a broken window in the back door, but nothing else seemed to be touched in the room. We followed Mitchell into the living room, where we both stopped and stared silently. Torn wrapping paper and empty boxes of various sizes littered the room, along with several partially unwrapped gifts. Our Christmas tree lay on its side amid the chaos.

I put an arm around my aunt, and Mitchell slid a hand under my hair and gently massaged the back of my neck, sending goosebumps along my scalp.

"The rest of the house seems to be untouched," he said. "I would guess we interrupted them when we pulled in the driveway. I don't think they even went upstairs, as a laundry basket with neatly folded clothes is sitting on one of the bottom steps. Did one of you leave it there?"

"I did," I said. "Sorry, Aunt Star." She liked things to be

orderly, but I wasn't as organized as she was.

"Don't worry about it. Sounds like that's helping us out here."

"Since I didn't plan to investigate any crimes tonight," Mitchell said, "I don't have a notebook on me. We'll wait for the others and then take inventory of what's missing."

Red and blue lights flashed through the sheer curtains, and the sirens stopped. Moments later, Frank and Jake entered through the garage, followed almost immediately by Darren.

The other policemen knew Mitchell, as he had helped with the other major crimes earlier in the year. He was officially employed by the Jefferson City Police Department, but they loaned him out when smaller towns needed assistance with big cases. Unfortunately for Cherry Hill— but fortunately for me—we often needed his help.

I surrendered Aunt Star to Darren, who pulled her in close and leaned down to murmur in her ear. The words sounded suspiciously like, "I love you." Though I was certain they did love each other, I had never heard either of them say the words, so I wondered if I heard correctly.

Mitchell filled the others in, and Frank took pictures of the scene while Jake dusted for fingerprints at the back door.

Darren asked Mitchell, "You okay with helping us out? I know you're on vacation."

"There's no way I'm not finding out who did this," Mitchell responded.

"I figured as much." Darren pulled out his notebook. "Let's get to it, then. Looks like the VCR is missing." He pointed to the top of our console TV, where the machine usually sat. "But the stereo is still here, which is interesting." He gestured across the room. "Anything else gone other than the gifts? We'll get to them in a minute."

"I don't think so," I said.

Darren poked his head into the formal dining room. "Doesn't look like anything was touched in here. Let's sit at the table while you list out the missing gifts."

Aunt Star and I followed him in while Mitchell stayed behind, gently moving pieces of wrapping paper around, searching for evidence.

"Unfortunately," I said, "most of the gifts my parents bought were here, as well as ours, since we're hosting the family celebration on Christmas Eve. There was a Cabbage Patch Kid for Jodie and a Teddy Ruxpin for Brandon." My seven-year-old niece and three-year-old nephew were arriving Monday afternoon from Chicago with their parents, my brother Rafe and sister-in-law Cari. The kids would be devastated if we couldn't find or replace their gifts in time.

"How do you spell Ruxpin?" Darren asked.

"You haven't seen the five thousand commercials on TV?" Aunt Star replied.

He shrugged. "I don't pay attention to toy commercials."

"R-U-X-P-I-N," I said.

Aunt Star added, "Also a Rainbow Brite, a Care Bear, some Transformers, a few G.I. Joe figures—though I think I might have seen some of those toys scattered around the living room."

"Hold up," Darren interrupted her, "I can't write that fast."

He caught up, and we rattled off a few more gifts for the kids.

"There was one of those new Nintendo things for my dad," I said.

Darren's eyebrows shot up. "Your dad?"

"He became addicted when we were at Rafe's house for Thanksgiving. He can't stop talking about it, so we all pooled our money to get him one. I had to drive to St. Louis to track one down."

"I'm jealous," he said. "What else?"

"Wait, you want a Nintendo?" Aunt Star asked him. "Why didn't you tell me?"

"You didn't ask what I wanted for Christmas. I guess you didn't get me anything." He gave her a fake frown.

She swatted his shoulder. "You know I got you something. More than one something, to be accurate."

"More than one?" He opened his eyes ridiculously wide. "I'd better go shopping again, then."

Aunt Star rolled her eyes, while I wondered if Darren bought her a ring. My aunt was fiercely independent, so I hoped if Darren planned to propose, it wouldn't come as a surprise to her. However, I desperately wanted them to get married, because he made her exceedingly happy, and she was still young enough at thirty-eight to give me some baby cousins.

Frank stepped into the doorway. "Neither of you ladies smoke, do you?"

"No," I said. "Why?"

"Found a cigarette butt with lipstick on it out back. Any female smokers visit you lately?"

Aunt Star and I looked at each other questioningly, and we both shook our heads.

"Bag it," Darren told Frank.

"Already did, boss."

"Find anything else?" Darren asked.

"Detective Crowe bagged a few things from the living

room. Don't know what, though."

"All right. Carry on." Darren returned his attention to his girlfriend and me. "What other gifts were in there?"

"There was an opal necklace for my mom," I said, "a man's watch, a few Nintendo games, some cassette tapes and videos—"

"Slow down," Darren ordered. "This is a lot of stuff." He cut a glance at Aunt Star. "Were *my* gifts under the tree?"

"No," she said, "I haven't wrapped them yet. They're in my closet."

"Whew." He swiped his hand across his forehead and grinned but then caught himself. "Sorry. I shouldn't be happy when most of the other gifts are gone."

Mitchell appeared in the doorway and leaned against the jamb with his thumbs hooked in his belt loops. My pulse raced as he held my gaze while he waited for the others to notice his presence. Heat rushed up my neck, and he grinned in response. Making me blush was one of his primary life goals.

Darren finally noticed him. "You need something?"

"I found a few interesting things. One, there are a few drops of blood on the carpet in front of the couch. Was that there before?"

My aunt and I shook our heads.

"You would think they'd wear gloves, though, right?" I asked.

"Have you ever tried to unwrap a present with gloves on?" he responded. "I can't imagine it's easy."

"Why did they unwrap the gifts?" Aunt Star inquired.

I replied, "I'd guess they only wanted to take the good stuff—whatever 'good stuff' means to them. Most of the gifts also would be easier to carry if they're unwrapped and out of the boxes."

"Excellent deductions." Mitchell smiled at me. "I also found the VCR remote among the mess, which isn't really a clue, but that will make the machine harder for someone else to use, which makes me happy."

I chuckled. "Me, too."

"We might be able to pull some fingerprints off it," Darren said.

"I bagged it," Mitchell affirmed. "I also found part of a poinsettia leaf, but I don't see any poinsettias in the house. Have you had any?"

"No," Aunt Star said. "That's weird."

"Indeed it is. That's all I've got so far. I'm not done in there, though."

He winked at me before heading back to the living room, and my face heated again.

Darren then pointed between Aunt Star and me. "What about the gifts you bought each other?"

"Not under the tree," I said. "We got tickets to see John Cougar Mellencamp at the St. Louis Arena in February."

"And you didn't invite me?" He gave Aunt Star his fake frown again.

"Nope," she said. "Girls only."

"I see how I rate," he said. "No Nintendo. No Mellencamp."

My aunt rolled her eyes. "I think you'll live."

A walkie-talkie squawked in the other room. Frank's voice filtered to us, but we couldn't make out his words.

"Boss," Frank said from the doorway a few seconds later, "there's been a break-in at the hardware store, too."

TWO

DARREN STOOD QUICKLY, bumping his head on the chandelier over the dining table as he did so.

My heart felt like it was in a vise as Frank continued, "Olivia is on her way to the store already." Olivia Pierce was the latest addition to the Cherry Hill Police Department. "Who else do you want to go?"

Darren rubbed his head with one hand and stilled the swaying light fixture with the other. "You and I will go while Mitchell and Jake finish up here." He leaned down to give Aunt Star a kiss.

"Where's the chief?" she asked him.

"Visiting his daughter in Oklahoma," he said over his shoulder as he strode out of the room. "He'll be gone all week." They wouldn't miss him much. The current Chief of Police acted more as a figurehead than anything else.

"Wait," I said weakly, but Darren was gone.

Aunt Star touched my hand. "You worried about Marty?"

I nodded. Marty James managed the hardware store in downtown Cherry Hill, across the street from First Community Church, where I was the secretary. The two of us had been friends until a couple months earlier, when some previously unexpressed feelings between us came to light. The subsequent ending of our friendship was still a painful memory for me.

Mitchell joined us at the table and scanned Darren's list. "You got me a Nintendo! You shouldn't have." He grinned at me.

I gathered my strength and gave him a smirk. "You wish. The Rainbow Brite is for you." He didn't yet need to know the watch was for him.

He put both hands over his heart. "I will cherish her for the rest of my days."

"You'll have to find her first."

His hands dropped to the table. "Right. I definitely have to solve this case now. I can't let Rainbow live with a thief."

I wished I could enjoy our banter, but I was too concerned about Marty. "Did they give any details about the hardware store break-in?"

"Only that the back door was smashed in."

I closed my eyes, and when I reopened them a few seconds later, Mitchell gave me a shrewd look and said, "I doubt Marty is in the habit of being there this late on a Saturday night."

"You never know."

He covered my hand and curled his fingers around mine. "Try not to worry. We'll find out what's happening soon."

A walkie-talkie squawked again, and Jake soon entered the room.

"There's been another break-in," he directed at Mitchell, "at Suzanne LaHaye's house. Darren told me to go over there, and he asked if you could join me after making sure these ladies are safe. None of the others can leave the hardware store right now."

My heart moved into my throat. What if Marty was hurt ... or worse?

Mitchell stood. "Go ahead. I'll be right behind you."

Jake disappeared, and Mitchell said, "I don't want to leave you two here alone, but I also don't want to leave the house unsecured with nobody in it." He looked at me. "Can you see if your dad will come over and cover up the broken window in the back door? Then both of you go stay at your parents' house tonight."

"You think we can't fix the door?" Aunt Star retorted.

"I'm one hundred percent certain you can. But do you want to? And do you have any plywood?"

"No," she said without needing to stop and think about it.

"Exactly. I'll wait to leave until I know Ron's on his way." He tucked Darren's notebook and pen into his shirt pocket.

I dug my keys out of my purse, slipped my house key off, and handed it to Mitchell. "If you get a chance to sleep tonight, the guest room is all yours."

We trooped into the kitchen, and I dialed my parents' number from the wall phone. Mom was unhappy with my lack of detailed explanation but promised she and Dad would come over as soon as they could gather up the supplies.

"Can we touch anything we want now?" Aunt Star asked Mitchell.

"Only in the dining room and upstairs. It's fine to touch the back door, as we've taken fingerprints and inspected it closely already. Leave everything as it is in the living room and kitchen. And don't go onto the back porch or into the yard."

Aunt Star nodded and headed upstairs, leaving Mitchell and me alone in the kitchen. He gathered me into his arms and searched my eyes. "Tell me how you're feeling about this."

"I'm mad, but this break-in isn't as unsettling as the last one. This time we know what the intruders were after. Last time we weren't exactly sure."

"I'm glad you weren't here when it happened." He kissed my forehead. "Or Starla."

"Me, too. I'll be glad to see the backside of 1985. This has been quite a year for Cherry Hill."

"Next year can only be better, that's for sure." He pulled me in tighter and smirked at me. "But you met me this year, so it wasn't all bad."

I went up on my tiptoes and gave him a peck on the lips. "You make an excellent point."

Mitchell loosened his grip on me. "I need to go."

"Be careful out there in the snow."

"It stopped a little while ago. The roads shouldn't be too bad, and it's only a few blocks to Suzanne's house."

"Good. I really hope Suzanne isn't hurt." Suzanne LaHaye was the choir director at First Comm. She and I weren't the best of friends, but I didn't want anything terrible to happen to her.

He placed a hand on my cheek. "When I get a chance, I'll call and let you know how she is, okay?"

I shifted my gaze from his eyes. "And Marty, too?"

He suppressed a sigh. "Yes, Marty, too."

"Let me give you my parents' phone number."

I plucked the notebook and pen out of his pocket and wrote down the number. Then he kissed me and headed out the door.

My parents soon arrived with a small piece of plywood and Dad's portable toolbox. Before Mom would let Dad board up the door, she made me tell them everything. After I ordered them not to touch anything in the kitchen or living room, I went upstairs to pack.

I gathered up my toiletries and dumped them into a duffel bag. Then I set a towel and washcloth on the guest bed for Mitchell. There was nothing I could do about clean clothes for him, as none of ours would come close to fitting his six-foot muscular frame.

Aunt Star sat on my bed while I finished packing. "Mitchell was nice about Marty."

I nodded but didn't say anything. My aunt knew the entire story about Marty—much more than Mitchell knew.

She cocked her head as she watched me decide which sleep clothes to take. "I haven't asked you this in a while, but do you have any lingering feelings for Marty?"

"I made the right choice with Mitchell."

I stuffed my flannel Christmas tree pajamas into my bag. My parents' house was always chilly in the winter.

She lightly grasped my wrist, and I stilled.

"I don't disagree," she said. "But you didn't answer my question."

I pulled my hand from hers and tossed a new pair of L'eggs pantyhose, some underwear, and my black pumps into the bag and zipped it up before responding.

"Yes, I know, but I don't really know how I feel about him." I sat next to her and looped my arm through hers. "I do know I hate how much I hurt him. Whenever I run into him around town, he won't look me in the eye, but he's always kind. I think that makes it even worse." Tears pricked behind my eyelids. "I wish he would be mean to me. It's what I deserve."

"It most definitely is not. You didn't do anything wrong, and he knows it. That's why he's kind to you. Well, and he's a good man and he cares about you."

A tear ran down my face, and I swiped it away. "I care about him, too."

"You should. He was a good friend and helped you through a tough time. It's hard losing a friendship, no matter the reason. You're being too hard on yourself, Becks. You didn't ask Marty to fall for you."

"Girls!" Mom shouted up the stairs. "You ready to go?"

"I'm still a girl at twenty-eight?" I asked my aunt.

"I've got ten years on you, but apparently my big sister thinks I'm still a girl, too." She moved to the doorway to yell, "We'll be down in a minute!" Then she turned to me. "Chin up. Marty's a grown man who can take care of himself. And you have an amazing boyfriend who loves you, so just remember that."

My jaw hit the floor.

"What?" she said. "You didn't know he is ridiculously in love with you? He maybe hasn't said it, but it's obvious to anyone who has seen him in your presence." She shook her head. "I can't believe he hasn't said it."

"Probably because—"

"You want to take things slow?" she interrupted. "Yeah, we need to have a chat about that as well, but that's a conversation for another time. Let's go."

I grabbed my green blouson dress from my closet, threw the duffel bag over my shoulder, and headed downstairs.

———

"WHAT ARE WE GOING to do about all the Christmas gifts?" Mom asked.

Mom, Aunt Star, and I sat at my parents' kitchen table in our pajamas eating popcorn, even though it was past midnight.

"We'll have to get a few more things for the kids, at least," I said. "As for the gifts you bought me, I'm fine with waiting to see if everything turns up. I'm guessing all you other adults feel the same. But we only have two days to get more gifts for the kids."

"A handful of the kids' presents were still there," Aunt Star said, "but I'm sure the Cabbage Patch Doll and Teddy Ruxpin were gone, along with the Nintendo. Do you think the gifts the thieves didn't take will need to be confiscated as evidence?"

"I don't know," I responded. "If we do need to replace some things, we maybe won't be able to get anything from the hardware store, depending on what happened there. We might find a few things at the dime store, and maybe we can find time to run to Jeff City or Columbia to the mall or Toys 'R' Us to see if they still have any Cabbage Patch Dolls or Teddy Ruxpins left in stock, though I doubt it."

"We can call the stores and ask, before we drive all that way," Aunt Star said.

"Good idea," Mom said. "I'll make some calls tomorrow after church. Now, who are our suspects?"

I replied, "It must be somebody who lives in Cherry Hill, don't you think? It seems like they knew which houses to hit to get the most bang for their buck ... so to speak." Aunt Star and Suzanne were two of the wealthiest people in town, which was well known. My aunt owned and ran the biggest and most successful real estate agency in the tri-county area, and Suzanne's late husband left her very well off thanks to his rental properties and life insurance policies.

Aunt Star said, "There's the possibility it could be someone we suspected of the bank robbery back in October."

Mom suddenly stood and left the room. Aunt Star and I gave each other curious looks, but my mother returned quickly with a notepad and pen and set them in front of me.

"We have Cory Hankins and Kimberly Banner." I wrote their names down. "Kimberly is back in town, after flunking out of college. I've seen her and Cory together a few times." Cory was a high school senior who had gone off the rails over the previous year.

"What about Zane Patrick?" Mom asked. "We thought he might have robbed the bank."

Zane had a history of breaking and entering. I added his name to the list.

"It had to be more than one person," I said. "I'm certain we interrupted the robbery at our house, or they would have gone upstairs and looked for jewelry or electronics or money or *something*. There wasn't a vehicle in our drive or on the street out front, which means they left on foot through the backyard, but they took much more than one person could carry."

We discussed a few more possibilities before Mom stood. "I can't stay up any longer. We'll continue this conversation over lunch at The Check tomorrow." We always ate lunch together at The Checkered Cloth diner across the street from the church after Sunday services.

I brushed my teeth and had finally gotten myself comfortable in my childhood bed when the phone rang.

"Beckett, it's Mitchell!" Mom called out from her bedroom a few seconds later.

I hopped out of bed and hurried to the kitchen phone in

my bare feet, wishing I had packed some slippers.

When I picked up the phone, Mom was speaking. "How's Suzanne?"

Mitchell responded, "She's shaken up but fine. Same thing happened at her house as at Beckett and Starla's, but they took a lot more stuff. Thankfully she wasn't home when it happened."

"I'm here now, Mom." I stretched the phone cord across the kitchen to the table and took a seat. "You can hang up."

"First I want to hear what happened at the hardware store," she said.

"Let me talk to Mitchell," I said. "I'll fill you in later."

"I simply want to know if everyone is okay," she said. "Sorry for being a caring person."

I sighed. "Fine, stay on. Mitchell, tell us what happened, so she can go."

"Unfortunately," he said, "everybody was not okay at the hardware store."

THREE

MY STOMACH DROPPED, and I felt like I might throw up.

Mitchell continued, "Darren found Marty unconscious in the sporting goods section, which had been partly cleared out along with some of the toys and power tools. It appeared he was knocked over the head with something, likely a baseball bat."

I choked back a sob. "Is he ...?"

"He's on his way to the hospital in Jeff City. They said he was conscious when the ambulance left, but he wasn't making much sense."

"Did anyone go with him to the hospital?" Mom demanded.

"Yes, his mom got there in time to ride in the ambulance with him. His dad was driving to meet them at the hospital."

Footsteps padded across the kitchen floor, and Aunt Star's small hand slipped onto my shoulder. "You okay?" she whispered as she pulled a chair next to me and sat.

I shook my head as tears trickled down my face.

"Marty?" she asked me. She must have heard Mom's end of the conversation.

I nodded. She jumped up to grab me a tissue and then rubbed circles on my back.

"It was good talking to you, Minda," Mitchell said by way of telling Mom it was time for her to hang up. "I'm sorry I don't have better news to report."

"Thanks for calling. We'll see you tomorrow?"

"Undoubtedly. Bye, now."

The line clicked when Mom hung up.

"Baby, I think he'll be okay." Mitchell's voice was full of compassion, which made me cry even harder. "He's a strong, healthy man."

"I h-hope so." I cleared my throat.

"Is Starla right there with you?"

"Yes."

"Good. I won't keep you, because I know you're upset. I wish I could be there, but we've got a long night ahead of us."

"I understand." I sniffled. "You have a job to do."

"I do. I'm sorry. I—" He sighed. "I'll see you tomorrow."

"Yeah," I whispered. "Good night." I sobbed silently.

Aunt Star took the phone from my hand and hung it up. Then she led me back to my room and tucked me in.

"You want to talk about it?" She perched on the edge of the twin bed.

I shook my head. "There's nothing to say."

"At least tell me what Mitchell said about Marty."

I recounted the conversation.

"I'm sure Marty will be fine, Becks," she said in a low voice so my parents wouldn't overhear. "Try not to worry about him. Do you think maybe you're so emotional about Marty because you're still upset about hurting him and losing his friendship a few months ago, and not because you have romantic feelings for him?"

I turned away from her onto my side. "I don't have the energy for this conversation right now. I want to sleep."

"You need to have this conversation, though." She moved

around to the other side of the bed. "You have to work through this. Mitchell knows you're more upset about Marty than you probably should be about a man you're not dating." She cocked her head to the side. "Are you taking things slow with Mitchell because of Marty?"

"Partly."

"Okay, we'll come back to the Marty issue in a second. What's the other part?"

"I'm afraid I'll want to try to fix Mitchell."

Aunt Star sighed. "You're not with Mitchell because you want to fix him. He's not Walter. He's not Jeff. He's not any of the string of other guys you've attempted to turn into better men ever since Billy Arbuckle broke your heart when you were seventeen."

"You didn't need to throw all my exes in my face." I wiped my eyes on my pillowcase.

"That's not what I was doing. I'm saying you deserve a man who's so much better than all those guys. And you seem to have found one." She smoothed a wayward curl back from my face. "Does Mitchell know about Walter and why you didn't date anyone for a couple years?"

I closed my eyes. "I'm not brave enough to tell him. He'll think I'm silly and weak."

"No, he won't, because it's not true." She touched my arm. "Becks, look at me."

I slowly opened my eyes and rolled onto my back.

"You did need to take a break from men when you moved back here, and there's nothing wrong with your reasoning for not wanting to jump straight into the deep end with Mitchell. But I think you've gotten it into your head you're never going to be able to choose a good man for the right reasons. You can't stay in that mindset any longer." She placed her hand over my heart. "Mitchell is a good man, and he loves you." He did love me. I was sure of it. And it scared the living daylights out of me.

She continued, "He's a strong, honest, thoughtful man who doesn't need fixing, as far as I can tell. You're holding back with him because you don't want to be in another unhealthy relationship, but in the process, you're making this one unhealthy for no good reason. It *can* be healthy, but you have to talk to Mitchell about all of this. Tell him why you've wanted to take things slow—all the reasons. But first you need to figure out how you feel about both him and Marty. He can't help you with that."

"I don't know if I can figure it out."

"Do you love Mitchell?"

Did I? I wasn't sure. And I'd been wrong about being in love before. "I don't know."

"If he were to walk into this room right now and say, 'Beckett Monahan, I love you with all of my being,' how would you respond?"

I closed my eyes. "I would cry."

"Why?"

"Because I couldn't say it back."

"Because you're scared, or because it's not true?"

"I'm definitely scared." I opened my eyes and looked at her. "Can our relationship really last? We still don't see each other very often. He's always running off somewhere else for his job. Even if we lived in the same city—even if we were married—how often would we be in the same place at the same time? I don't want my husband and the father of my children to be gone all the time."

"Surely he won't have this traveling detective job forever."

"I don't know. He really enjoys going to all the different places and helping the departments out."

"Sounds like the two of you need to talk about it. See if he'd be willing to stay in one place for your sake."

"But I don't want him to sacrifice his career for me."

"That's not your decision, sweetie. And the alternative might be him sacrificing you. My guess is he'd pick you."

"Yes, and then I'd feel guilty for the rest of my life that I kept him from the job he wanted."

"This is why you two need to talk about it. Maybe he truly wouldn't mind having a job where he stays in one place most of the time." She gave me an uncharacteristically tender look. "I think you might love him. If you didn't, you probably wouldn't care so much about him hypothetically making huge sacrifices for you."

I put my forearm over my eyes while I contemplated everything she said. "You might be right."

"Oh, I'm definitely right."

I removed my arm from my face and gave her a playful shove. She balanced herself quickly enough not to fall off the bed onto the floor.

"Seriously, though," she said, "If you decide for sure I'm right, I think you should tell him."

I looked away from her for a moment but then locked eyes with her again. "Do you tell Darren you love him?"

"Every single day."

My eyebrows shot up.

"So does he. Just because we don't say it in public doesn't mean we don't say it. When you love someone, you should tell them as often as possible."

A smile spread across my face. "You loooooove him."

She tried to hold back her own smile, but she failed miserably, and her face flushed. "I do. And you changed the subject. We're not talking about me and Darren."

"We should."

"Not tonight. I need to get some sleep. So do you, but I doubt you'll get much with all this running through your mind."

Tears filled my eyes. "Thank you for making me talk about this, even though I didn't want to."

"I'll always be here for you. I love you, kiddo," she said and kissed my cheek.

"Love you, too, old lady."

———

SUNDAY MORNING WAS A logistical dance, with four of us sharing one bathroom while getting ready for church. Aunt Star typically didn't attend services, but as it was Christmas week and Mom gave her a guilt trip about it, she made an exception. Thankfully for our morning preparations, though, she wasn't going to Sunday school, so she didn't need to finish getting ready as soon as the rest of us.

My aunt called the police station when she first woke, but she was unable to talk to either Darren or Mitchell. Darren was off chasing down a lead, and Mitchell had gone to our house to get a few hours of sleep. The officer she spoke to promised to tell one of them to call us when they could.

While Mom showered and Dad read the Sunday paper in his recliner, Aunt Star cornered me in my room. "How are you feeling about everything we talked about?"

"Better. I decided I need to get past the Marty situation. But I'm not sure I'm one hundred percent in love with Mitchell yet," I said as I sat at my old child-sized vanity and applied my makeup. "I don't know how much my feelings have been influenced by the excitement of us having to sneak around for so many months. And I'm certain he feels more strongly about me than I do about him."

I looked down at my hands. "I'm also not sure I fully trust him. Maybe I haven't told him all that stuff not because I don't trust myself but because deep down I don't trust him for some reason."

"Has he done or said anything to make you think you can't trust him?"

"No, but I've never told him anything this big. What if he doesn't deal with it well?"

"There's no way to find out other than to do it. You going to try to talk to him today?"

I had lain awake for hours thinking and praying about what I was going to say to him, how I would say it, and what he might say back. I looked at my aunt through the mirror. "If he has time. I'm not sure he will." My stomach was going to be in knots until I could get him alone long enough to talk through everything.

"Stop making yourself nervous thinking about all the ways he might respond." She knew me too well.

"I can't."

"Try. It's not helpful."

"I'll do my best, but I don't think it will work." I paused while I swiped green eyeshadow on my eyelids. "I want to know how Marty is, though, regardless of all the rest of it. I do care about him." For the first time in two months, talking about him didn't make me want to cry, which was a good sign I might be able to fully move on.

"I know you do. So do I, for that matter. Why don't you call his parents' house or the hospital and see what you can find out?"

Aunt Star left the room to take her shower, and I found Mom in the kitchen making pancakes. She wore a pastel green housecoat, and a towel covered her hair.

"What are you doing?" I asked.

"Making you breakfast."

"But you need to finish getting ready."

"I will after this," she said. "You need to get to church earlier than your dad and I do."

"I would offer to help, but I'm going to call around and see what I can find out about Marty."

"Good. I want to know, too."

I pulled the phone book out of the cabinet by the phone and looked up his parents' phone number. I let it ring ten times before giving up. Then I dialed the hospital, and the front desk connected me to his room phone. A woman answered, but the voice didn't sound like Marty's mom or sister.

"Is this Marty James' room?" I asked.

"Yes, can I help you?" Since the woman didn't introduce herself, I assumed she was a nurse.

"This is ... his friend, Beckett Monahan. I'm calling to see how he's doing."

"It's kind of you to call. He's doing great this morning. They want to keep an eye on him throughout today, but he should be able to go home in the morning."

They? If this woman wasn't on the hospital staff, who was she?

FOUR

"I DON'T MEAN TO sound rude, but who are you?" I asked the woman on the other end of the phone.

"Patty Conroy. Marty's girlfriend."

"His girlfriend?" I squeaked out before I could stop myself.

Mom spun to face me, spatula in hand. Pancake batter dripped onto the floor.

"Yes. Can he not have a girlfriend?"

"Um, he can, but I figured I would know about it if he did." Though I wouldn't have heard about it from him. This unexpected turn of events left me with a strange feeling in my stomach—not exactly nausea, but definite unease.

Mom raised an eyebrow at me, and I shrugged. She turned back to the stove.

"Patty, please give me the phone." Marty's voice sounded irritated in the background, which was surprising, as he was not easily perturbed.

"I guess you're not as good of friends with him as you thought, Beckett," the woman said triumphantly.

Then the line clicked, followed by the dial tone. I held the phone in front of my face and stared at it.

"What was that all about?" Mom said over her shoulder.

I put the phone back on the hook. "I have no idea. A woman named Patty, who claims to be Marty's girlfriend, answered the phone. She was rude to me, and Marty told her to give him the phone, and she hung up."

"Sounded like you were a little rude right back. Did this woman at least say how he's doing?"

"He'll be fine. Should come home tomorrow."

"That's great news."

"Yes."

Mom gave me a strange look. "Why are you just standing there?"

I shook my head in a failed attempt to clear it of my swirling thoughts. "I don't know." Then I crossed the kitchen and headed down the hallway.

"Where are you going?" Mom yelled. "Your pancakes are almost ready."

I ignored her and knocked on the bathroom door.

"What?" Aunt Star demanded from inside while Mom hollered my name from the kitchen.

"Can I come in?"

"Hang on."

I tapped my foot while I waited. When Mom yelled at me again, I informed her I'd be right back.

"All right," Aunt Star finally said. "Come ahead."

I slipped inside the cramped space with my towel-covered aunt.

"This had better be good," she said as she ran a comb through her short, wet hair.

"I don't know if 'good' is the word for it." I relayed my strange phone conversation in a voice low enough to not be overheard if Mom was listening in the hallway.

"So Marty has a girlfriend." She said it as a statement, not a question. "How do you feel about that?"

"I don't like her. I can't imagine why he'd date someone who could be so rude to one of his friends."

"That's not what I'm asking, and you know it."

I put the toilet lid down and sat on it. "I don't like it."

"Is this a case of 'if I can't have him, nobody can have him'?"

"Maybe."

"How would you feel if you found out Mitchell was dating someone other than you?"

My hands fisted. "I would be enraged."

"That's pretty telling. You're not enraged about Marty, are you? Maybe a little bit jealous."

"I'm not jealous!"

She raised an eyebrow at me.

"Okay, fine." I slumped down. "What is *wrong* with me? I have an amazing boyfriend, yet I'm jealous of another man's girlfriend."

"At least now you know he has moved on."

"I guess."

"You have to move on, too, Becks—for everyone's sake. There's no point agonizing over a man who no longer has feelings for you. Now get out of here so I can get ready and your mom will stop hollering."

The phone was ringing when I left the bathroom.

"Beckett, it's for you!" Mom yelled. "And your pancakes are getting cold."

I entered the kitchen and Mom handed me the phone. "Marty. He won't tell me anything." She stalked out of the room.

"Hi," I said tentatively.

"Beckett, I am so sorry about that call."

"I ... uh, well, I didn't realize you had a girlfriend."

"I don't."

"Then who in the world was that woman?"

"I took her on *one* date a few weeks ago." He huffed out a breath. "I knew I shouldn't let my mom set me up with anyone, but she wouldn't stop badgering me about this woman she met who just moved to Taylorville, so I gave in. The date was fine, though I didn't have much desire to go out with her again. But now Patty won't stop calling and won't take no for an answer. She showed up here this morning a few minutes after my parents left. After she hung up on you, I sent her on a wild goose chase to find me some red JELL-O, which I've already been told doesn't exist in this hospital, but I'm certain she'll do her best to find some anyway."

"Wow," was all I managed to reply to his monologue as my body relaxed. I hadn't realized how tense I was.

"Wow to which part?"

"All of it." And my see-sawing emotions.

"Right? I can't get her to leave. Will you call Kyle and see if he'll come up here and help me out?" Kyle Korte was my former classmate and Marty's current roommate. "Please?" He sounded desperate.

"Sure. Now tell me how you're feeling."

I stretched the phone cord across the room to the kitchen table and sat in my usual spot, where Mom had left my plate full of cooling pancakes.

"My head feels like it might explode, but otherwise I'm not feeling too bad. I should have a full recovery."

"That's great to hear. Do you feel well enough to tell me what happened at the hardware store last night?" I took a bite of lukewarm pancake.

"Detective Crowe hasn't filled you in? I know he's helping with the case." I could tell by the tone of his voice he was really asking whether I was still dating Mitchell.

"He called late last night to tell me you'd been hurt during the robbery, but he didn't know much else. And right now he's getting a couple hours sleep over at my house." I cocked my head. "Speaking of my house, how did you know to call me here instead of there?"

"Suzanne called earlier to interrogate me. She told me about the break-ins at her house and yours. Are you and Starla all right?"

"We're a little shaken up, but we'll get over it."

"I'm sure you will. You've been through much worse."

"Unfortunately."

"Yes. Anyway, when nobody answered at your house just now, I assumed you went to your parents' house overnight."

"Excellent guess." I hoped he didn't leave a message on our answering machine that Mitchell could have overheard. "Now tell me what I need to know so I can help find the people who did this to you and who took my niece's and nephew's toys."

"Beckett, that's your boyfriend's job, not yours. You need to stay out of it—stay safe."

"Don't you tell me what to do, Marty James."

He chuckled, and I smiled at how easily we seemed to be falling back into our friendship.

I added, "But I do appreciate your concern for my safety." I stood and moved to the far corner of the kitchen where I was least likely to be overheard. "Marty?" I said softly.

"Yes?"

"I don't like it when we're not friends."

"Me, either. I've missed you."

My heart felt like it was being squeezed. "Can we do this, though? Can we just be friends?"

"I'd like to try, but I'm not the one who's dating someone else. I don't want to put you or Mitchell in an awkward situation. He has to be okay with it, too." He paused. "Have you told him what happened?"

"Kind of."

"I'm not exactly sure what that means, but I'll trust your judgment on what you think he needs to know. And you need to know if we do restart this friendship, I promise to never touch you again, and I will keep any potential future non-platonic feelings to myself."

I wondered if that meant he didn't currently have any non-platonic feelings for me. I wasn't sure what I wanted the answer to be. "Okay. I'll talk to Mitchell."

Mom re-entered the kitchen and tapped her watch. I glanced at the clock on the wall, which told me I was going to be late if I didn't hurry up.

I said to Marty, "Back to the robbery, I think your recovery will go faster if you tell me what happened last night."

"Yes, I can see the correlation," he said wryly. "But I know you're like a dog with a bone when it comes to these investigations, so I'll tell you."

"Make it quick, because I need to get to church."

"Yes, ma'am."

I finished eating my pancakes while Marty talked.

"I was working late in the office and fell asleep at my desk, but I woke up when the back door crashed open downstairs. It took me a few seconds to figure out what was happening, and I rushed out without thinking about finding something to use as a weapon. By then, the thieves had made their way upstairs and were more than surprised to see me. One of them grabbed a baseball bat from the rack near the top of the stairs and rushed toward me. The next thing I knew, I was in an ambulance."

"I'm so sorry. Did you get a good look at them? How many of them were there?"

"The store lights weren't on, but the office light and the thieves' flashlights gave me a glimpse of some of them. There were at least four people. All teenagers or close to it, I'm pretty sure, by the way they moved. The only one I got a decent look at is the one who hit me. It was a high school kid I've seen before, but I don't know his name. Any minute now, Officer Pierce should arrive with a yearbook to see if I can pick him out."

"Are they worried the thieves might try to hurt you again to keep you from talking?"

"There's a Jefferson City police officer outside my door."

"Glad to hear it. Anything else I need to know?"

"I don't think so, and I hear Patty talking to someone in the hall, so I better go. Thanks for calling. I can't tell you how much I appreciate it."

I smiled. "It's what friends do. And I'll call Kyle right now."

We hung up, and I called Kyle, who promised to head directly to the hospital and get rid of Patty. Kyle was a world-class flirt, so I had no doubt he could sweet talk Patty into leaving.

Then I rushed down the hall and knocked on the bathroom door again.

"What now?" my aunt asked.

"Let me in."

She opened the door, and I quickly told her about my latest conversation with Marty.

"First of all," she said while putting on her foundation, "I fully believe that in theory men and women can be friends. But things can get sticky if one person has romantic feelings the other person doesn't or can't return. Unless you know where he stands on his feelings for you—even though he has promised not to act on them—I don't know if being friends with him is a good idea, as long as you're dating Mitchell."

"Maybe it's not, but I don't want to not be friends."

"What do you think Mitchell will say about it?"

"He probably won't like the idea, but I don't care. I don't like the idea of him deciding who my friends are—or aren't. He doesn't get to make that decision for me."

My aunt grinned at me. "I have taught you well." She pointed her mascara wand in my direction. "But that still doesn't mean you and Marty being friends is a good plan."

"Well, I'm not going to blatantly ask Marty if he still has feelings for me, so there's nothing I can do about knowing where he stands."

"Want me to ask him for you?"

"We aren't in seventh grade," I said, "so no."

"Okay, but I'm going to ask *you* if this latest conversation with Marty gave you any more insight into how you feel about him."

"I don't know. I was relieved when I found out he wasn't dating Patty, but I don't know if that's because I don't like the thought of him dating anyone or because she was rude and annoying and I don't want him to date her specifically." I took a deep breath. "However, I'm going to put it all behind me and focus on Mitchell. I like him a lot, and there's no point in trying to juggle two men."

"You're still going to talk to Mitchell, though? You'll tell him about Walter and everything with Marty?"

"I have to. I won't be able to live with myself if I don't. I need to tell him the whole truth about all of it."

––––––––

FOR ONCE, I WASN'T annoyed when Suzanne LaHaye accosted me the moment I stepped foot in the church.

"Honey, are you okay?" She pulled me into a hug against her plump bosom.

I patted her back and then extricated myself from her embrace. "Yes, I'm fine. And you?"

"Furious. How dare those kids break into my home and take my belongings—*and* my grandson's Christmas gifts!"

"Yeah, I'm not too happy about the Christmas gift situation, either." I headed toward the church office, and she followed. "So what exactly happened at your house?"

"Your detective hasn't told you everything?"

"I haven't been in touch with him yet this morning. I'm not sure he would tell me everything, anyway."

"You need to learn to exert pressure on people to get what you want, Becky."

I decided to try it. "You know what I want right now?"

"What?"

"For you to call me Beckett." Suzanne never called me by my full name, instead continuing to address me by my childhood nickname.

"It's hard to remember not to call you Becky." She trailed

into the office behind me.

"Why don't you practice right now?" I dropped my purse into my desk drawer and sat in my rolling chair.

"Okay ... Beckett." Suzanne squeezed herself into one of the guest chairs across from my desk.

"See how easy that was? Now, tell me everything."

"Well, I called Marty this morning, and I went to the police station and hounded them until they would tell me anything of importance. The police think my house was hit first, then yours—but they were interrupted—and then the hardware store. Nobody else reported a break-in, so the thieves probably got scared after they knocked Marty over the head, and they ended their spree."

I looked at the clock. "What else can you tell me? Choir rehearsal and Sunday school start in ten minutes, and I'm subbing in third grade this morning."

"I should already be in the choir room warming up, so I'll hurry." She leaned toward me. "Did the thieves unwrap all the gifts at your house, too?"

"Yes."

"In amongst all the wrapping paper at my house, the cops found a man's glove—*a glove!* And you know what? It had initials written on the inside tag in permanent marker." She shook her head. "How dumb can you be?"

"What were the initials?"

"C.H."

FIVE

MY EYEBROWS SHOT UP.

"My thoughts exactly," Suzanne said with a nod, "C.H.— Cory Hankins."

"We don't know for sure. Those are common letters. I should ask Trixie what other high schoolers have those initials." I groaned and palmed my forehead. "Trix. I can't believe I haven't called her."

Trixie Wallace had been my best friend since birth, and she taught math at Cherry Hill High. She would be furious I hadn't thought to call her about the break-in.

"What else do you know?" I asked Suzanne. "And hurry it up so I can call Trixie before Sunday school."

"They found five sets of footprints in the dusting of snow in the parking lot behind the hardware store. Sounds like those kids don't have a functioning brain between them." She tapped her head with her pointer finger.

"How in the world did five teenagers sneak around in a couple of backyards and the parking lot behind the hardware store and not be seen?"

"Maybe they *were* seen," Suzanne said. "The cops didn't say there were any sightings, but you're right. It wasn't even very late when it happened. Most people wouldn't have been in bed yet." She heaved herself out of her chair. "Is there anything you know that I need to know before I go?"

"Do you have any poinsettias at your house?" I asked.

"Yes, I have quite a few. They're so festive. Why?"

"The police found a poinsettia leaf at our house, but we don't have any. I bet it got caught on one of the thieves' clothes at your place and then fell off at mine. That might be how they determined your house was hit first."

"Could be."

Before she left, I asked, "What's my name?"

She cocked her head to the side as if she were thinking hard about it. Then she thrust a finger into the air. "Beckett!"

I grinned at her. "Great job."

I dialed Trixie's number as the door clicked shut behind Suzanne.

"Beckett Lee Monahan, why didn't you call me before now?" she demanded by way of a greeting.

"I'm sorry. It was a stressful night."

"Aw, Beck. I'm sorry. I shouldn't have yelled at you. You okay?"

"Yes."

"I'll tell you, I was more than a little surprised when I called your house earlier and Mitchell picked up while I was leaving a message on your answering machine. Then I called your parents' house, but the line was busy. So tell me what happened."

I gave her a brief rundown of events.

"And now I have a question for you," I said. "Which high schoolers have the initials C.H. other than Cory Hankins?"

"Why?"

"The police found a glove with those initials in it at Suzanne's house."

"That's convenient. Let's see. There's Chris Hinkle. Wait,

was it a men's glove or women's glove?"

"Men's, but that doesn't mean a woman can't wear them, so tell me the girls, too."

"All right. Also Celia Hunt ... and Curt Hartman."

I wrote the names on a piece of scrap paper.

"Is Chris a boy or girl?"

"Girl. I can't think of any others at the moment. Also ..." she trailed off.

"What?"

"Have you heard anything about Marty this morning?"

I normally told my best friend everything, but I didn't have the time or the inclination to tell her about the morning's phone calls, because she would want to dissect everything, so I only said, "Yes, he's going to be fine."

"I'm so happy to hear that."

I checked the clock. "Sorry, but I need to run. I'm subbing in a kids' class with Veronica, and I'm late. She's going to kill me." Veronica Coker, the pastor's wife, was my co-substitute teacher in the third-grade classroom for the morning.

"She won't. But she will almost definitely yell at you."

I laughed. "You're probably right. Talk to you later."

"Keep me posted."

I rushed down the hall to the classroom, and sure enough, Veronica gave me an earful when I arrived. "Beckett, I thought I could count on you to not be late for once. These children are driving me batty."

The kids were indeed rambunctious, but it was nothing I couldn't handle. Within a minute, they were all settled down and working on a Christmas craft.

"How did you do that?" Veronica asked. "Not a single one

of them would listen to me."

"The hard-nosed approach doesn't really work with kids these days."

"It worked with my two."

"They must be special," I said diplomatically. "Aren't you going to ask me how I am?"

"Well, you're here and you're not crying, so I would assume you are fine."

"I am."

"Good." She gave me a brisk nod. "Have you solved the crime yet?"

"Of course not. I can't do it without my trusty sidekick." I smiled at her.

She rolled her eyes, but she couldn't keep a smile off her face. Veronica helped me solve the other cases throughout the year. We had even grown fond of each other in the process.

"Tell me what I need to know, then," she said.

I gave her all the details in fits and starts, in between leading the kids' activities and keeping them under control. Again, I avoided mentioning I had talked to Marty. She knew about what had happened between us, and while she typically gave good relationship advice, I wasn't ready for anyone else's opinion.

When I mentioned Cory Hankins' name a few minutes later, she said, "I can tell you Cory didn't do it."

"How can you possibly know that?"

"Harold and I were at the Kiwanis Club Christmas party last night. Cory was there, too, until at least 10:30 when we left."

Mitchell and I had arrived back at my house around 10:00,

so she was right. Cory wasn't one of the thieves.

I asked, "Why was a high school boy at the Kiwanis party?"

"His mom told me he was grounded, and they didn't trust him to stay home while they were out, so they made him come with them."

"I'll admit I'm relieved he wasn't involved."

"Me, too." She smirked at me. "We'd never win conference without him." Cory was the star on the varsity basketball team.

"I didn't know you were such a fan."

"We've been going to the home games this year. I enjoy it more than I thought I would."

I could totally see Veronica getting into the games— probably too much.

After Sunday school, I stopped to chat with the youth minister, Greg, in the foyer outside the sanctuary when a hand slipped around my waist. I turned in surprise to discover a smiling Mitchell.

He gave me a chaste kiss on the cheek and then turned to Greg. "Hey, man. How's it going?"

I held my breath.

"Fantastic," Greg replied. "It's good to see you."

His response seemed genuine, and I exhaled. Greg had asked me out several times over the past year before Mitchell and I officially started dating, and I had turned him down each time. Historically, he wasn't Mitchell's biggest admirer, and the feeling was mutual. The two men shook hands before Greg excused himself.

I ran my eyes up and down Mitchell's body. He wore the same jeans as the day before, but he was now sporting a red button-up shirt that clung to his muscular frame. I slid a hand up his arm. "Where'd you get the shirt?"

"Darren. It's a little long and tight, but it's clean." Darren was six-foot-five and lean, so I was surprised the shirt fit at all. "I didn't want to wash my clothes at your house in case I had to leave quickly. Didn't want to be caught without anything to wear."

I tried not to dwell that scenario, so I focused on the shirt. "I like it." I ran my fingers across his chest, where the material was stretched almost to its breaking point, and then looked up at him. "Why are you here?"

He put his hands on my waist. "You're not glad to see me?"

"I'm ecstatic to see you." I looped my arms around his neck. "But I figured you'd be working."

"Since I'm technically on vacation, I thought I'd spend at least one hour of the day with my favorite girl." He kissed me again—not so chastely. I knew I should pull away instead of making a scene in the church foyer, but I couldn't bring myself to do so.

"Get a room, you two." Aunt Star materialized at our side, looking classy as usual in a burgundy skirt suit and white silk blouse. Her jacket collar sported a jeweled Christmas tree pin. "Catch the thieves yet?" she asked Mitchell as he reluctantly let go of me.

"Not quite. Shouldn't be long, though."

"Really?" I looked up at him.

"I worked as hard as I could overnight in an attempt to finally solve a crime in this town before you do." He winked at me. "Darren and Frank are questioning a suspect as we speak."

"Is it the kid who hit Marty? Was he able to identify him from the yearbook?"

Mitchell's forehead creased. "How in creation did you know about that?"

I bit my lip. "I talked to Marty before church."

"Oh, did you?" He raised one eyebrow and gave me a speculative look.

"Mitchell!" Dad clapped a hand onto Mitchell's shoulder. "Good to see you, son."

"You, too, sir."

"No need to call me sir."

"Yes, sir ... I mean Ron."

Dad asked him a question about the investigation as a teenage girl appeared by my side.

"Is that Mitchell?" Tiffani whispered.

"Yes."

"Ooo." She wiggled her eyebrows. "He's yummy ... for an old guy. And he's *built.*"

I laughed. Mitchell was more than twice her age, but Tiffani was as boy crazy as any eighth-grade girl.

"Hey, there's Celia Hunt," she said. "I've never seen her at church before."

I whipped my head in the direction Tiffani was looking and spotted a tall, sullen-looking teenager standing with an older couple who occasionally attended services. The girl was undoubtedly their granddaughter and had been dragged to the Christmas service against her will.

The organ came to life, blaring out "I Heard the Bells on Christmas Day," which was our cue to take our seats. Tiffani rushed off, and I took Mitchell's hand.

We entered the sanctuary behind Celia and her

grandparents. As they turned into a row near the back, I sucked in a breath when I noticed a bandage wrapped around the girl's right hand.

"Mitchell." I squeezed his hand as we continued up the aisle toward my family's usual pew.

"Hmm?" He glanced down at me distractedly.

"That girl back there," I pointed with my head, "has a bandage on her hand. And her initials are C.H."

He stopped in his tracks, suddenly on high alert. "Which one? Show me."

I pointed her out as surreptitiously as I could.

"What's her name?"

"Celia Hunt."

"Go sit with your family. I'll join you in a few minutes." He strode back up the aisle.

"Where's he going?" Aunt Star asked as I took a seat next to her.

"I'll tell you later," I whispered as Pastor Coker welcomed the congregation.

We were singing "Joy to the World" when Mitchell slipped into the pew next to me.

"How did you know about the C.H.?" he murmured in my ear as he slid an arm around me.

"I know everything," I whispered back. "Did you call Darren?"

"He's sending Frank over here to take her in for questioning when the service is over. We're not going to make a scene, if you're worried about that."

"I wasn't."

Mom reached around Aunt Star, poked me in the arm, and shushed us.

"Sorry," I mouthed to her. I could feel Mitchell silently laughing beside me.

————

TRUE TO MITCHELL'S WORD, Frank didn't make a fuss as he approached Celia's family after the service. He even wore plain clothes—a thoughtful detail I appreciated.

"You heading to the station?" I asked Mitchell as we watched them head out the door. "Or going to lunch with us at The Check?"

"Will you be very upset if I don't go to lunch? I promise to see you again later today."

"I won't be upset. But I will hold you to that promise." I put my hand on his chest and took a deep breath. "There's some things we need to talk about."

His eyes searched mine, and I detected a hint of unease in his gaze. "Okay."

I pulled his head down for a kiss to try to reassure him. He kissed me back but drew away after a few seconds. His hand squeezed mine before he walked away, and my heart lodged in my throat.

Aunt Star patted my arm. "It will all work out the way it's supposed to."

I nodded as Veronica approached us.

"Looks like Harold and I are joining you for lunch," she said. "Mitchell's not staying?"

"No, he needs to go back to the station for a while." I decided not to tell them about Celia, in case we were wrong.

"Do you know why Frank was here?" Veronica asked. "Looked like he walked out with the Hunt family."

So maybe I would fill them in. "I'll tell you at lunch." That way I wouldn't have to retell the story to Mom, who would demand to know all the details.

Fifteen minutes later we all reconvened at The Check. Dad and Pastor Coker sat across from each other at one end of the table, giving us ladies the opportunity to easily talk amongst ourselves.

Callie Collister, our favorite waitress and Aunt Star's lifelong best friend, took our drink orders. "Wish I could stop to chat about what happened last night," she said, "but we're swamped."

"Hopefully you'll have time before we leave," I said. Callie often helped us fill in the gaps of our investigations.

She hurried away, and I told the others everything I learned from Suzanne, as well as what was happening with Celia Hunt.

"Did I hear you mention Celia Hunt's name?" Callie asked after she took our food order.

"Yes. What do you know about her?" I asked.

Callie glanced at the nearby tables and then squatted down at the end of ours. "Her parents split up a few months ago, and she's temporarily living with her grandparents. She's been quite a handful, from what I hear."

"Do you know who her friends are?" Veronica asked.

"I've seen her smoking in the parking lot behind the diner with Mark Glass," she said.

Since The Check was two doors down from the hardware store, they shared a parking lot—the same one the thieves had left footprints in the night before.

"Why would they hang out back there?" Mom wondered.

"Mark works at the dime store after school a few nights a

week." Links' Five and Dime was on the corner, beyond the hardware store.

"I wouldn't think he'd be involved in the robbery then," I said. "He would have recognized Marty's pickup in the lot and known he was in the store."

Callie shrugged. "Maybe Marty wasn't parked in the lot. Or maybe the kid isn't very observant."

"The thieves did make a lot of mistakes," Mom said. "They obviously didn't plan very well."

"Callie, can I use the phone to make a local call?" I jerked my head toward the phone behind the counter.

"Sure." She stood. "And I need to go put your order in."

I followed her across the diner and dialed the police station. I insisted on speaking directly to Mitchell. The officer on the phone argued with me since Mitchell was conducting an interview, but I channeled Suzanne and didn't back down.

"Baby, what's wrong?" Mitchell asked in a concerned voice when he finally came on the line.

"I'm fine. Ask Celia about Mark Glass. I think they're dating, which means he might be involved, too."

"Thanks. She hasn't mentioned his name. In fact, she hasn't said much of anything. Unfortunately, she's a minor, which means we can't grill her as hard as we'd like."

"Also," I said, "she's a smoker, so the cigarette butt from our house might be hers. Maybe you can match the lipstick color on it to hers or something. Or at least act like you can, when you're talking to her."

"Dang, you're good at this."

I smiled. "I know. Now go back in there and get that girl to tell you everything."

"I'll do my best."

"I sure hope Darren had the sense to let you be the 'good cop' with her. I have it on excellent authority even teenage girls find you extremely appealing, especially in that skin-tight shirt you're wearing. My advice? Roll up the cuffs—while she's watching."

"Beckett Monahan, I am *not* going to pretend to seduce a teenage girl."

My face heated, but not for the usual reason. "I didn't think that comment through, did I?"

"Indeed you did not. But it was educational, nonetheless," he said teasingly.

My face flamed even hotter. "Well," I said in a fake put-upon manner, "if you insist on being a man of impeccable character, I guess I can't complain. But I will tell you this: Darren's not getting his shirt back if I have anything to say about it."

He was still laughing when he hung up the phone.

SIX

"THE TOY STORE AT Columbia Mall has two Cabbage Patch Dolls," Mom said on the other end of the phone. "They won't hold one for me, though. Should I send your dad up there to get one or not?"

"I don't know." I sat cross-legged on my bed and smoothed my hand over the flowered Laura Ashley bedspread. "I have a feeling the police might wrap this thing up today and find all the stolen items. But if they don't, we'll be in trouble. What about Teddy Ruxpin?"

"There's not one to be found anywhere within a two-hour drive—at least not at stores that are open on Sunday. You think Marty has any in stock?"

"I doubt it," I said. "Even if there were some, Mitchell mentioned the burglars took some of the toys from the store."

"I think I will go ahead and send your dad to Columbia. It'll get him out of my hair for the afternoon, and he'll have plenty of time to get back before the Christmas program at church tonight. I'll have him pick up a few other smaller gifts for the kids, too, just in case. We can always return it all if we get the original toys back."

"Tell him to get a Rainbow Brite." If we got the other gifts back, I was giving the extra one to Mitchell.

"Why?"

I thought fast. "Because Jodie really wants one. I don't

want her to be disappointed."

"All right. Have you girls heard from Mitchell or Darren?"

"Not in the twenty minutes since we last saw you."

"No need to get snippy with me."

I sighed. "I'm not snippy."

"I beg to differ."

Arguing with my mother was almost always a losing game, so I let it go.

"I feel useless right now." I slouched down. "I can't think of anything I can do to help solve this crime."

Aunt Star came in and joined me on my bed. "We could always drive around town," she said loudly enough for Mom to hear. "Scope out the houses of the two kids we think might be involved, and see if we discover anything else that might give us a clue."

"Excellent idea," I said. "We'll take Mom's car, since ours are both pretty noticeable."

"Do I get any say in this?" Mom asked.

"Don't you want to come?"

"You bet your boots I do. But not until I get your father out the door. He doesn't need to know anything about it."

"I hope he didn't hear you say that."

"He's in front of the TV watching football. I could dance naked on the coffee table, and he wouldn't notice."

That was a visual I hoped I could scrub from my mind.

"You sure he's going to leave his recliner to drive to Columbia?" I asked.

"He will do what I say, and he will do it with a smile."

I didn't doubt the first part, but the second was debatable.

"Well," I said, "you have fifteen minutes to get him out the door, because that's when we'll be there."

I hung up and immediately called Veronica to see if she wanted to join us.

"Harold's snoring away in his chair, and he'll likely still be there when it's time for dinner, so he won't even know I'm gone. Swing by and pick me up."

When I hung up with Veronica I asked my aunt, "You know who else we need to call?"

"Who?"

"Marty—to find out the name of the kid who knocked him out." I pulled a phone book out of my nightstand drawer.

"You keep a phone book in your room?"

"Why? You don't?"

"I don't call people from bed if they're not close enough to me that I don't already know their number. That's weird."

"I'm not always in bed when I make a call from in here. Why do you care anyway?"

She shrugged and grabbed the phone book from me. "You call the hospital, and I'll find the kids' addresses."

"I need the hospital number first."

She turned to the yellow pages at the back and rattled off the number.

While I waited to be connected to Marty's room, Aunt Star flipped to the H's. "What's Celia's grandpa's name: Arnold, Charles, or Henry?"

"Arnold."

She grabbed a pen and the Sears Wish Book off the mess on top of my dresser, wrote the address on a corner of the catalog cover, tore it off, and shoved it in her pocket.

"You miss me already?" Marty asked when I identified myself.

"You're hilarious. Still doing okay?"

"They've got me on some good pain medicine now, so I am hunky dory, A-OK, excellemundo."

I stifled a giggle. "I am very glad to hear that. Do you have your wits about you enough to tell me the name of the kid who hopefully finally knocked some sense into you?"

"Now you're the one who's funny."

I waited for him to answer my question, but he didn't.

"I'm always a barrel of laughs," I finally said. "But are you going to tell me the kid's name?"

"Oh. Ted Bundy."

"Ted Bundy," I repeated slowly. "You sure?"

"Ninety-five percent."

"How about the other five percent? What are those brain cells telling you?"

"Ted ... Danson?"

"Try again."

Instead, he began singing the theme song to *Cheers.*

"What is happening on the other end of the phone?" Aunt Star asked.

"He's on drugs," I replied. "Marty," I said into the phone. "Marty!" I repeated louder.

He abruptly stopped singing. "Why are you yelling at me?" I could almost see him pouting.

"Is anyone there with you right now?"

"Like who?"

"Oh, I don't know," I couldn't keep the sarcasm out of my voice, "maybe your parents or Kyle?"

"Kyle's a good guy. Annoying, but a good guy."

I allowed myself to giggle at his truthful statement, though I hoped Kyle wasn't there to hear it. "I know. Is he there?"

"He got that awful woman to go away."

"I'm glad."

"She's a terrible kisser."

My mouth twitched. "Good to know. Is Kyle there?"

"Why? You want to talk to him?"

"I do."

"He's not here."

I rolled my eyes. "Is your mom there? Or your dad?"

"Nope. Only me. Me-me-me," he sang in a high-pitched voice.

I covered the mouthpiece with my hand and asked Aunt Star, "Do you know of a high school kid named Ted something?"

"Ted Posey. You know him, too. He lives a few doors down from your parents."

"That kid is already in high school?" In my mind, he was still the obnoxious six-year-old down the street who liked to make rude comments about me and my boyfriends.

"Sure is."

"Marty?" I said into the phone.

"Yeppers?"

"Was it Ted Posey?"

"Was *what* Ted Posey?"

"The kid who hit you over the head with a baseball bat last night."

"Of course," he said imperially. "I told you that already."

"Well, you tried your best. Okay, I gotta go. Can you hang up the phone?"

"Been doing it all my life."

"Great. I'll talk to you later."

As I was hanging up, I heard his voice again, so I put the phone back up to my ear. "Did you say something else?"

"Yes, indeedy." He didn't elaborate.

"Well, what was it?"

He chuckled. "Did you just want to hear me say it again?"

"Hear you say what?"

"I love you."

My entire being stilled.

"Beckett, are you still there? Beckett? Beckett?" he parroted. "I like saying your name."

I couldn't make my mouth form any words.

"Beckett?" He said once again. "Hmm. I guess she's gone. I'll just have to tell her again later."

The dial tone buzzed in my ear as Aunt Star waved a hand in front of my face.

"What are you doing? I can hear the dial tone." She plucked the phone from my hand and hung it up. "What did he tell you?"

I turned my panicked eyes to hers. "H-h-he s-s-s-said ..."

"He said *what?*"

"That he loves me."

My aunt's eyebrows shot to her hairline. "Oh, Becks." She grabbed my hands. "He didn't know what he was saying. He's all drugged up."

"Yes, and those drugs are like a truth serum." I stared blankly at the wall.

"Well, it sounded like he couldn't get Ted's last name right."

"Yeah, but he doesn't know Ted. He probably forgot his name." I put my head in my hands. "What do I do now?"

"What do you want to do now?"

"Go back in time and not call him!"

"Unfortunately time travel is not an option. But sitting

here and hashing it all out isn't an option, either, unless you want your mom in on this." She stood and pulled me up with her. "She's expecting us at her house any minute, and if we don't show up, she'll demand to know why. I hate to say it, but you need to put your big girl pants on and do your best to pretend this didn't happen—at least for now."

———

WE PICKED VERONICA UP on the way to my parents' house. She was dressed all in black, though why, I couldn't fathom, since it wasn't dark outside.

Dad's pickup drove away from my parents' house as we approached from the opposite direction. Instead of pulling into the driveway, I continued down the street.

"Where are we going?" Veronica demanded. She scooted to the middle of the backseat and stuck her head in between the front seats.

"Making a slow drive-by of the Posey house," Aunt Star explained, since I wasn't in a talkative mood.

"Why?"

"Ted Posey is who hit Marty last night."

"Ohhhh. Which house is it?"

I stopped right in front of it.

"Don't stop!" Aunt Star said. "At least pretend we're not gawking."

Christmas lights twinkled from the tree in the front window, and a van sat in the driveway.

"They have a van," I needlessly observed to the others as I inched my car forward.

"All the better for hauling five teenagers around town

along with all the stuff they stole," my aunt said.

"My thoughts exactly," Veronica said. "Why would the van be here, though, instead of down at the police station getting fingerprinted and searched or something?"

"Maybe they already did that. It's been about four hours since Marty gave the name to the police."

"There's a shed out back," Veronica said. "Looks like a good place to store stolen goods."

"I'm sure the police would have already checked it," Aunt Star said. "Becks, turn around and go back to your parents' house."

"Beckett," Veronica said, "you've barely said a word since I got in the car. What's going on?"

"I can't talk about it now." I wanted to cry or throw up or both, but we had a crime to solve. "Please don't mention anything to Mom."

I expected her to argue with me, but she didn't.

When we headed back down the street, Mom was backing her car out of the one-car garage. I pulled in beside her, and we all piled out of my car and into her blue Ford Granada.

"Why did you drive down the street?" she asked.

Veronica explained about Ted.

"That must have all happened after we left for church." She craned her neck to look at Aunt Star next to me in the backseat. "How did you not hear anything? Surely there was a bit of a ruckus down there when the police came."

"No idea." My aunt shrugged. "Maybe they didn't use the sirens. And I wasn't in the front part of the house, so I didn't have a view of the street."

"Where are we going?" Mom asked.

Aunt Star gave her the Hunts' address. We drove by, and

the driveway was empty. The drapes on the picture window were open, but no lights appeared to be on inside.

I needed to start talking before Mom got suspicious. I took a deep breath and determined to focus on the case instead of the men in my life. "The family must still be at the police station," I said.

The house had a carport, not a garage, so I wondered if there was a storage shed in the backyard that wasn't visible from the street.

"Stop the car," I said.

Mom pulled off to the side of the road a couple houses down.

"I'm going to go see if they have a shed."

"No, you're not," my mother said.

"They're not even home. It'll be fine."

Mom reached back to lock my door and then started driving again. I unlocked the door and opened it. She slammed on the brakes. "Child, what in the blazes are you doing?"

I jumped out before she could start driving again. "You know what I'm doing. Anyone coming with me?"

Veronica exited the car and marched down the street. I joined her.

"What's our plan?" she asked.

"We'll knock on the door, in case any neighbors are watching. Then we'll go around back, as if searching for a back door to knock on."

Veronica climbed the steps on the tiny front porch ahead of me and rapped on the metal frame of the screen door. Unsurprisingly, nobody answered. She then followed me through the carport and into the backyard, where a small shed stood a few feet from the back of the house. The door was padlocked. I rattled it, but it didn't come loose.

"Hey, what do you think you're doing?" came a deep voice from the backyard next door.

I dropped my hand. "Nothing."

"Don't look like nothing." A large man wearing ripped pants and a stained sweatshirt ambled toward us smoking a cigarette. He pointed the cigarette at Veronica. "Aren't you that preacher's wife?"

I wondered how Veronica would handle him.

"Indeed I am," she said. "My friend and I came to pay the Hunts a visit, but we couldn't rouse anyone at the front door. We thought we'd come try the back."

"That ain't the back door."

I jumped in. "I was thinking about getting a new padlock for my own shed," I thought about it for half a second, so it wasn't technically a lie, "and I thought I'd see what kind they have."

"Don't seem likely," he said. "I have half a mind to call the police, 'specially considering them burglaries last night."

SEVEN

"NO NEED FOR THAT, SIR." Veronica took me by the elbow and backed me toward the corner of the house. I stumbled on a rock, but she steadied me before I fell. "We haven't done anything wrong."

"Looks to me like you're trespassing," he declared.

"Hard not to trespass in order to knock on someone's door," she responded. "Plus, you seem to be trespassing, too."

I held my breath. This was not a man to be trifled with.

His eyes narrowed slightly, and he blew a stream of smoke out through his nose as he perused us. "You two get on out of here." He waved his cigarette in a circle. "Go on."

Veronica pulled me around the corner of the house, and we walked briskly back to the car.

"Well?" Mom said when we got in.

"Drive," I commanded.

Shockingly, she didn't argue and took off down the street.

"Where to now?" Mom asked.

Aunt Star gave her directions to the Glass home, and Veronica filled them in on our encounter with the neighbor.

I said, "I don't think the stolen stuff could be in that shed. It was too small, and it's undoubtedly where they keep their lawnmower and other yard stuff, because there's nowhere else to put it."

"Nobody will be getting out of the car here," Mom stated when we reached Mark's home in one of the nicer subdivisions in town.

Five cars sat in the driveway, along with a few on the street. If it wasn't almost Christmas, I'd be suspicious by the amount of activity at the house. I glimpsed a two-story detached three-car garage in the backyard.

"Looks like they've got plenty of storage space," I said.

"I'm sure the police will check it if they think Mark is a viable suspect," Aunt Star said. "Let's go back home."

"Wait," I said. "What about Celia's parents? Callie said they split up but didn't say why Celia isn't living with either of them. What if one or both of them are still in town, or they at least still have a place here? Maybe Celia would store the stolen goods there."

"There were two other Hunts in the phone book," my aunt said. "I don't remember the addresses, though."

"I'll head back home, then, and we can check," Mom said.

"And when we get there, I'll call the police station and see if anybody will talk to me," I said.

I was put immediately through to Mitchell when I called.

"We just got a call about two suspicious women hanging around the Hunt house, one of whom walked with a limp," he said, "and the other was identified as 'that pastor's wife.' You happen to know anything about that?"

"Why would I?" I asked innocently.

"Oh, I don't know, maybe because you have a history of doing that sort of thing."

"Do I? I don't recall ever being arrested for trespassing."

He snorted. "Not for lack of trying. Seriously, though, stop it."

"Mitchell ..."

"I know—don't tell you what to do ... or not do. But please promise me you'll be careful."

"I'm always careful."

"You are absolutely not." He paused. "You going to be home this evening?"

"I'll be at church for the Christmas program from about 6:45 until 8:30."

"Ah, yes. Can I come over after that?"

"Of course." My stomach clenched at the thought of the conversation we would be having, especially after Marty's revelation. "If I'm not mistaken, you'll need a place to sleep tonight. You're welcome to stay again." I wasn't sure he'd want to after we talked, though.

Veronica raised an eyebrow at me from across my parents' kitchen table. I had a strong feeling she wouldn't approve of him spending the night, no matter which bed he slept in.

Mitchell said, "I'll need to head home afterward for a decent night's sleep and some clean clothes that fit properly. As much as you appreciate the shirt I'm wearing, the buttons are starting to strain. I need my own clothes."

I sighed. "If you must. By the way, have you found the stolen items yet?"

"No, but we do currently have four teenagers in custody at the station."

"Four? Who's the fourth?"

"I don't think I'm going to tell you. We don't need you snooping around their house."

"That's not even on my radar."

"You're a terrible liar. And you haven't asked me for the name of the kid who knocked Marty out. I assume that means you found out?"

"Yes." I bit my lip.

"From Marty?"

"Yes."

"You've talked to him twice today?" he said in a much-too-casual tone.

"Yes," I said once again.

I knew his jaw was clenched without even seeing him.

"Who called who?" he asked.

I wasn't sure which answer he preferred, but I wasn't going to lie. "I called him *at the hospital,*" I emphasized, reminding him of the circumstances.

Mom gave me a speculative look from across the room. My gaze skittered away from hers.

"Okay," he said. "Calm down."

"Don't you tell me to calm down."

Veronica gave me a thumbs-up.

"Beckett ...," Mitchell said in a long-suffering tone.

I mentally counted to ten so I wouldn't say something I shouldn't.

"Wrap it up," Aunt Star whispered to me. "We're wasting daylight."

"Well," I finally said to Mitchell, "if you're not going to give me any more names, I'll let you get back to it."

"Please don't do anything reckless." At least he said please.

"Who, me?" I replied. "I'll see you tonight." I hung up before he could give me any more orders.

The other women knew better than to comment on my end of the conversation, so they avoided my gaze.

Aunt Star said to me, "Your mom says Henry Hunt is

Celia's dad, so we're headed to his last known address from the phone book. Come on."

We trooped back out to the car and headed across town. I told them what Mitchell said about the suspects.

"How can we find out who the fourth kid is?" Veronica asked.

An idea came to me. "Let's drive by the police station and see if we recognize any of the cars in the lot. The kid's parents are likely there."

Mom made a quick detour by the station, but it was fruitless. None of the cars jogged any of our memories, so we headed on to the other Hunt home. The house had an un-lived-in look to it. A shutter hung at an odd angle from a front window, and the storm door glass was shattered yet still somehow intact. Multiple fresh-looking tire tracks ran through the dead, overgrown grass and around the side of the house. An ancient car sat on cinder blocks under a free-standing metal carport, though I couldn't imagine why anyone felt it needed protection from the elements.

"Pull over," I said to Mom.

"No." She hit the gas so I wouldn't risk opening my door again. "If you're going to skulk around another house, you're going to do it after dark when you won't likely be seen again." She made a sharp turn. "Actually, I have a better idea. You're going to tell your boyfriend about that house and let the police deal with it."

"But don't you want us to solve this crime?"

"I don't care who solves it," she said. "I do care that nobody else gets hurt. We're going to the station, and you're telling Mitchell. Consider this a Christmas gift to both me and him."

Though I wasn't excited about facing Mitchell, knowing he'd almost certainly detect there was something wrong, Mom was on a mission, and I couldn't stop her.

When we reached the police station, Mom held onto my arm the entire way inside. I wasn't sure what she would do if I tried to make a run for it, but since my limp would hinder my escape, I didn't attempt it.

She marched me straight past the front desk—and the woman sitting behind it—and into "the pit," the large room with the officers' desks. Mom spotted Mitchell sitting at the desk in the chief's office in the back corner, and she steered me that way, but Frank stepped into our path.

"Minda, Beckett, can I help you with something?"

"Out of my way, Frank," Mom said. "We need to talk to Detective Crowe."

Frank looked at me, and I nodded. He stepped aside but eyed Mom warily while Mitchell watched our approach with a neutral look. Mom nudged me into the office and closed the door behind me. I was surprised she didn't stay to ensure I told Mitchell everything he needed to know.

Mitchell leaned back in his chair and crossed his arms. "What's this all about?"

I perched on the edge of the uncomfortable metal chair across from him. "My mom is making me tell you something."

"Oh, is she?"

I nodded.

"About the investigation or about something else?"

"The investigation." Thankfully she didn't know about the "something else," and neither would he at the moment if I could help it.

He uncrossed his arms and leaned his elbows on the desk. "I'm all ears."

I told him about Celia's dad's house. He listened intently, his expression giving away nothing.

"Did you check that house already?" I asked.

"No. We've been a little busy around here."

"Did anyone *think* to check there?"

He sighed. "No. We would have eventually, I'm sure."

"Will you go check it now?"

He crossed his arms again. "If we don't do it immediately, are you going to go back over there yourself?"

I studied his eyes. "No. I'm going to let you do it."

"Really?"

"Really. Merry Christmas."

He laughed. "I like your mom."

"Why? Because she can get me to do things you can't?"

"That should make me *not* like her, but I'm glad someone has a little control over your impulses." He gave me an indecipherable look. "Are you okay?"

I looked directly into his eyes and nodded.

"Good, but I gotta tell you, what's not okay is how warm it is in here."

My forehead wrinkled. "It's actually kind of cold."

"You sure?" He unbuttoned one of his shirt cuffs.

I giggled when I realized what he was doing, but the laugh faded as he slowly rolled up his sleeve. His eyes never left mine, and I tried to hold eye contact but watching his arm muscles at work was too mesmerizing. Heat flooded my face as he repeated the process with his other sleeve.

"You sure you're not warm? Your face has turned the color of this shirt."

I covered my cheeks with my hands. He smirked at me and then stood, rounded the desk, pulled me up into his arms, and kissed me thoroughly. I melted into him, thoughts of anything—and anyone—else completely obliterated.

"Seems like someone else also needs help controlling their impulses," I murmured against his lips when we paused to take a breath.

I felt him smile. "Our audience is helping to keep me in check."

My head whipped toward the window into the pit in time to watch several grinning faces swiftly turn away from us. Mitchell ran a finger down the side of my crimson neck, causing me to shiver.

"I hate you." I gave him a mock glare.

"I'm one thousand percent certain you don't," he said with a grin. He tipped his head toward the window. "They're pretty sure, too."

———

"IT'S DRIVING ME BONKERS that I don't know what's happening." I paced the floor in our living room, which was clear of both debris and blood stains. A handful of still-wrapped gifts sat under the upright tree. Warmth filled my chest when I realized Mitchell's time at our house that morning had been spent cleaning more than sleeping. It was also a good reminder he was running on very little sleep.

"I doubt they're in any danger," Aunt Star said from the love seat. "I can't imagine anyone was in Celia's dad's house, even if the thieves stored the stolen items there."

"I still want to know what's going on," I retorted.

"Sit down. Your pacing is driving me bonkers."

I sat on the couch and jiggled my leg up and down. "We can't even watch a movie to distract us, since the VCR is gone."

"All right, that's it," she said and stood. "Let's get out of here. I'm not going to be able to deal with you otherwise." She pulled me to my feet. "Get your coat on."

"Where are we going?" I asked when I slid into her sports car.

"Around."

"Around?"

"We'll drive *near* the Hunt house and see if our men are there."

"What if one of them sees us? It's not like anyone can miss this car."

"I'm free to drive around my own town anytime I dang well please. Darren Turley cannot stop me."

"Speaking of Darren ..." I turned the radio down, muting the sounds of Lionel Richie crooning "Say You, Say Me."

"Let's not."

"Oh, yes. It's your turn."

"I'm thinking you need to talk about Marty," she said as she backed out of the driveway. "You've not said a word about him since we left home earlier."

"I don't want to talk about him. I don't want to think about him. I shouldn't have to. I shouldn't even be in this situation. If he weren't under the influence of prescription drugs, he would have never said what he did."

"But he did say it."

"And I'm going to try to forget it."

"That won't be part of your conversation with Mitchell?"

I groaned. "I don't know. But now we're going to talk about you and Darren." I turned toward her. "You love him." "I do."

"What will happen if he gives you a ring for Christmas?"

She gave me a sharp look. "He won't."

"I think he might."

"He won't, because I told him not to."

My jaw dropped. "You what?"

She kept her eyes focused straight ahead. "I'm not ready to get married."

"You're thirty-eight years old."

She shrugged. "That's neither here nor there. Being ready for something so monumental has nothing to do with age."

"It might if you want to have kids." I was nervous mentioning her age again, even if indirectly, but the fact needed to be stated. "Not that you technically need to be married for that."

She gripped the steering wheel forcefully. "I fully realize both of those things, but I don't want kids."

My jaw dropped again. "Are you serious?"

"As serious as I ever could be."

I touched her arm. "Why have you never said?"

"Because people think it's unnatural." She clenched her teeth before asking. "Do you think so?"

"No. I wouldn't say it's unnatural. Uncommon, maybe."

She cut a glance at me. "You don't think I'm weird?"

"Oh, I definitely think you're weird, but not because of that."

She took a hand off the steering wheel long enough to flick my leg.

"Does Darren want kids?" I asked.

"He says he's fine without them." She took a deep breath. "But what if he changes his mind?"

"What if *you* change *your* mind?"

"I won't. If my biological clock hasn't started ticking by now, I'm pretty sure it's never going to."

"Does Mom know?"

"She does."

I managed to keep my jaw from dropping once again. The two weren't particularly close. I was surprised Mom knew something so personal about her sister that I didn't know.

She continued, "She straight-up asked me a few years ago. And believe it or not, she understands. I've never had a maternal inkling, which nobody knows better than she does."

"Wow."

"Wonders never cease."

"Is this why you're not ready to get married? Because you don't want to feel like you're trapping Darren into a life with no children?"

She sighed. "It's one of the reasons."

We passed Marty's house as we headed out into the snow-dusted countryside. Aunt Star didn't seem to notice, or she would have turned the conversation back to him.

"Where are we going?" I asked.

"Nowhere. Anywhere. I don't know. I can't have this conversation while I might accidentally see Darren."

"He loves you *so* much."

"I know." She gave me a sad smile.

"That shouldn't make you sad."

"It usually doesn't."

"I know you don't need to be married to have a happy and fulfilling life. But don't you want to marry Darren? Don't you want to see what life could be like with him?"

"What if it's not any better than my current life?" She paused. "What if it's worse?"

"What if it's ten times better? There's no way to know without trying it."

"I won't marry Darren just to try out marriage. I love him too much to do that to him. Plus, if I ever get married, I plan for it to be forever. When I give my word, I keep it. And I'm not ready to make such a huge commitment yet."

We were both silent for a while as we sped through the hills surrounding Cherry Hill.

"Would you live with him? Would that be enough of a trial?" I took a deep breath. "If I moved out of your house, would you ask him to move in?" I wasn't sure what I wanted her answer to be.

"No," she said without hesitation.

"Why? You don't have any religious objections against it."

"Living together isn't the same as marriage. There's no lifetime commitment involved. It would feel different. I also don't know if I want to live with someone full-time. I don't always play well with others."

"You live with me full-time, and we get along fine."

"We're family. And we each have our own lives. It's different than if I were living with a man. Plus, I don't think this town is ready for two of its most visible citizens to 'live in sin.'"

"Surely you don't care what the town thinks?"

"Not usually, but I don't want to hurt Darren's reputation or affect the business of any of my agents at the office. That wouldn't be fair to them."

There was nothing I could say to convince her. In fact, I didn't want to convince her. If she ever decided to get married—to Darren or anyone else—she needed to come to that decision entirely on her own.

"I will support you whether you ever choose to get married or not. You know that, right?"

She reached over and squeezed my hand. "Of course I do."

"But I feel like I must also tell you I would fully support you marrying Darren Turley, if you decide that's what you want to do."

"Thank you."

I turned the radio back up. Dionne Warwick and her friends were singing "That's What Friends Are For."

Aunt Star laughed. "Well, isn't that perfect timing?"

I giggled and sang along at the top of my lungs. When the song ended and a commercial came on, I turned the volume back down, leaned my head back against my seat, and watched the countryside fly by in the waning twilight.

Suddenly, I sat bolt upright. "Stop the car!"

EIGHT

AUNT STAR SLOWED DOWN but didn't stop. "Why do you want to stop?"

I turned in my seat and craned my neck to look behind us. "Did you see that ancient barn back there?"

"No. What about it?"

"There was a Ford Ranger parked outside it, and a man was carrying a box from the pickup to the barn. I think he's the fifth thief!"

She pulled off the road onto a narrow gravel lane. "What are the odds of that? Even if we go back, do you think we're going to be able to stop him?"

"At least drive back by and let's get another look," I pleaded.

She backed out and slowly headed toward town. As we popped up over the top of a hill, the small pickup pulled out onto the road, heading in the same direction as us.

"Do you have a pen and paper?" I needed to write down the license plate number, but I had failed to grab my purse before we left home. I opened the glove compartment and rifled through it.

"There might be a pen in there. Otherwise, check my purse."

I found what I needed and wrote the number on an old receipt. I also wrote down a rough description of the guy based on what I could see.

"What now?" Aunt Star asked.

"Stay with him."

"He's going to know we're following him."

"Not for a while. It won't be strange out here in the country. When we get to town, follow him for two or three turns. Then we'll run by the police station and give them the license plate number and tell them which way he's headed."

Aunt Star kept a safe distance between her sports car and the pickup. We trailed him as he made two turns after we got to town.

"I think I know where he's going," she said.

"Me, too." We were almost to Celia's dad's house.

The truck's left turn signal came on as we approached a stop sign. It started to turn, but then the vehicle jerked back straight and took off like a shot.

"What in the ...?"

"Police," my aunt said. She pointed to her left, where two police cruisers and Mitchell's truck were parked two blocks down outside the Hunt house.

"Follow him!" I yelled. "Go! Go!"

"No." She turned left, zoomed down the street, threw the car into park behind one of the police cars, and leapt out. She looked around frantically for a second and then raced toward Darren, who had just stepped out the side door of the house. She gesticulated wildly as she spoke to him, and I rushed to join them.

I thrust the receipt toward Darren. "Here's the license plate number."

"But we found the stolen goods here," he said. "Thanks for the tip, by the way."

"You're welcome. Are *all* the stolen things here?"

"We don't know yet. We still need to log everything."

I waved the receipt in his face. "I think you need to check this vehicle out. Have you figured out who the fifth person is yet?"

Mitchell's voice came from behind me. "I thought you weren't going to come over here."

I turned to face him as he strode across the yard. "I didn't."

He gave me an incredulous look.

"I mean, I'm here, but not for the reason you think."

"What's the reason?"

Aunt Star explained.

"The guy meant to drive down this street," I said, "but he changed course when he saw the police cars. There's something fishy going on with him, even if it has nothing to do with the robberies."

"We *are* still missing one culprit," Mitchell said. "None of the rest of them will give him up."

Darren's forehead wrinkled. "Why were you two driving around the countryside?"

"We felt like it," I said quickly—too quickly.

Mitchell's eyes narrowed. "You weren't following up on some tip you failed to tell us about?"

"Nope. Just out for a drive."

He gave me a sharp look, and I held my hands up.

"I swear, officer," I said with a Southern drawl, "it was only an innocent drive."

He rolled his eyes but nodded. Then he glanced at Darren, and they held a brief, silent conversation with their eyes before he focused on me again. "We'll look into it." He took the receipt from my hand and turned his head toward the house. "Frank!" he bellowed.

Frank poked his head out the side door. "You called?"

"Come with me back to the station. There's something we need to look into."

———

"I CAN'T BELIEVE MITCHELL didn't let me go to the station," I said to my aunt as she lay on my bed while I dressed for the church Christmas program.

"I can't believe you thought it was a possibility," she replied.

I stuck my tongue out at her and then hummed along to "Last Christmas" as it played on the radio.

"Why don't you get a boombox instead of listening to your crappy clock radio?" Aunt Star asked.

"I don't mind it," I said as I pulled on a pair of knee-high stockings.

"Do you know what you're going to say to Mitchell tonight?"

"Not exactly." I stepped into a pair of black pants. "I kept rehearsing it in my head earlier in the day, but that made me nervous. So I'm trying not to think about it. I don't want it to sound rehearsed anyway. I want it to come from the heart."

"Are you going to tell him what Marty said?"

"I don't know what you're talking about," I said flippantly.

"That's the way you're going to play it? Pretend it never happened?"

"I don't know if I'm going to tell him, okay? I'll have to wait and see."

"But you still want to be with Mitchell?"

I paused to truly think about it. I had no good reason not to be with him. While I cared for Marty, and there was at least some level of attraction there, I wasn't in love with him. And though I wasn't sure I loved Mitchell yet, I enjoyed being with him, and our physical attraction was off the charts. "Yes, I want to be with Mitchell."

"You sound confident in your decision, so I'll support it."

I slipped a red, white, and green striped sweater over my head, and Aunt Star sat up.

"You are not wearing that."

"What's wrong with it?" I demanded. "It's fun!"

"You look like a wacko candy cane." She paused. "No offense."

I widened my eyes at her. "Some taken."

"You need to look sexy tonight, not fun." She stood and tried to pull the sweater back off me.

I held firmly to the hem. "You want me to look sexy for church?"

"No, for Mitchell, you ding-dong."

"But he won't be there."

"You didn't think he'd be at church this morning either, I bet. Plus, what if he's here waiting for you when you get home?"

She was right. I let go of the sweater, and she yanked it off me a little too forcefully. Then she steadied my teetering body and cringed. "Sorry. I got a little carried away there over your fashion crime."

"You're forgiven, but don't do it again. I'm not even going to attempt to pick out something else." I pointed at my walk-in closet. "Get in there and find me something semi-sexy that won't send Veronica into convulsions."

She emerged a minute later with a silky green button-up shirt.

I shook my head. "I wore that to the class reunion."

"You're allowed to wear a shirt more than once."

"I was wearing it when someone was *murdered.*"

"If I recall correctly, that was also the day Mitchell kissed you the first time."

My face heated at the memory, and I cleared my throat.

"Exactly," she said. "You're wearing this shirt." She slipped it off the hanger and tossed it at me. "It's totally sexy, but Veronica won't be able to find a single thing wrong with it."

———

THE CHURCH YOUTH GROUP was singing a slightly off-key version of "Silent Night" near the end of the Christmas program when movement along the side aisle caught my attention in the semi-darkness. I smiled when I recognized the creator of the distraction. I scooted closer to Mom and patted the empty spot by my side.

Mitchell climbed over a few pairs of legs and settled in next to me. He didn't say anything, likely for fear my mother would shush him again, but he slid his hand onto my knee and squeezed it. Tingles shot up and down my leg, and I had to focus hard to keep still. I slipped my hand under his and intertwined our fingers.

I had a hard time paying attention to the rest of the program, as I was anxious to get home and get our talk over with while also dreading the prospect. Mitchell lightly caressed my thumb with his own, as if attempting to calm my nerves, though he couldn't know how much I needed it.

When the service ended, Suzanne made a beeline for us. "Have you found my stuff yet?" she demanded of Mitchell.

"Yes, ma'am."

I turned to him. "All of it?"

"We think so."

"Did you catch all the kids?" Suzanne asked.

"We sure did."

"The last guy ...?" I raised my eyebrows.

"Yes, we caught up with him."

"Well, who were they?" Suzanne demanded.

"Most of them are minors, so I shouldn't identify them," Mitchell replied.

"I'm going to find out anyway," she retorted.

"I know." His lips twitched. "That's why I don't feel bad about not telling you."

Suzanne narrowed her eyes at him but then burst out laughing. "I like this one." She pointed at him while looking at me. "He's a keeper ... Beckett."

I beamed at her and then turned my head to find Mitchell giving me an adoring look. He slipped an arm around my waist and pulled me securely against his side. "This one isn't half bad, either." He kissed my temple.

Suzanne batted a hand at us. "You two are too cute! Especially in your red and green, looking all Christmassy."

Her eyes lingered on Mitchell's chest, and I choked back a giggle as he dug his fingers into my side.

"When are you celebrating Christmas at your house?" Mitchell asked her, and her gaze snapped back up to his.

"Tuesday—Christmas Eve."

"Good," he said. "We should be able to get the Christmas

gifts back to you before then. Stop by the station tomorrow afternoon, and we'll figure out what you need now and what we can hold onto a little longer as evidence."

"Excellent. I'll see you then." She patted his arm and trundled away.

———

AUNT STAR WAS GONE when we arrived at the house. She had headed over to Callie's house to give us some privacy, with orders for me to call her the second Mitchell left.

Mitchell sat on the couch and tugged me down next to him.

I twisted toward him. "I need to be able to look you in the eye when I say this."

We adjusted our bodies so we were facing each other, and I held his hands loosely in mine. My lips trembled when I tried to speak, and he said, "You can do this. Whatever it is, we'll work through it, all right? You can trust me with anything you need to say."

His words gave me the courage I needed. "I've never told you I was engaged before I moved back from St. Louis to Cherry Hill."

"Engaged ... to be married?"

I nodded. "His name was—is—Walter. I broke it off a few months before the wedding."

"Why?"

"You know how I love to help people?"

"It's one of the thousands of things I love about you."

My heart clenched, and I shook my head. "Don't say things like that until I finish this story."

"Okay." His thumbs stroked the back of my hands.

I gently pulled my hands away from his. The brief flicker of hurt in his eyes pained me, but his touch was too distracting. I needed to be able to fully focus on what I was saying.

"You know the story of how Billy Arbuckle broke my heart before my senior year of high school. And you know I dated Jeff Jenkins after that."

Mitchell nodded.

"I dated Jeff partly to get back at Billy, but also because he was fun. We had been friends our whole life, and we enjoyed spending time together. We both made it clear we didn't want a serious relationship, but we did have some very deep conversations. He was struggling with some things in his life, and to be honest, he was kind of a mess. I thought I could help him ... fix him ... turn him into the man I knew he could be. In my mind, he needed me. I was more than willing to try to fix him, and he didn't try to stop me. Oh, how I wish he had tried to stop me."

"Beckett, you were seventeen. And there's nothing wrong with wanting to help people."

"I know. But the problem was I kind of *did* fix Jeff, which gave me a sense of power. He and I broke up after we graduated and I moved to St. Louis for business school, like we had planned to do all along. And then I did the same thing with a few other men, but each time, I feel deeper. I wanted to stay with them—keep fixing them, keep making them better. Those other guys each eventually broke up with me ... until Walter."

I looked away from Mitchell's tender gaze.

"Tell me about Walter."

"Walter had many issues—lots of complex problems I wanted to solve for him, and he was more than willing to let me try, while taking none of the responsibility for himself. My parents and Aunt Star didn't like him. I mean, my dad likes everybody, but not Walter. Trixie tried to talk me out of marrying him. But I was so focused on my role as Walter's helper, his fixer, that I ignored all their warnings."

"But you did break up with him," he said. "How did that happen?"

"He was arrested for something idiotic, and he blamed me. He said it was my fault because I allowed him to do it."

Tears filled my eyes. Mitchell's hands fisted, and I knew he was aching to comfort me, so I held my hands out to him again and he grasped them firmly.

"I bailed him out, but that was the beginning of the end for me. I finally saw him for who he really was—not who I hoped he could be. He wasn't happy when I called off the engagement. In fact, at first he acted like it didn't even happen. He kept planning the wedding, even though there wasn't going to be a bride. The whole thing was maddening. It was Aunt Star who finally convinced him it was over. She never would tell me exactly what she said to him, but it did the trick." I looked down at our hands. "I can't believe I was such an idiot."

Before I could register what was happening, I was on Mitchell's lap with his arms wrapped tightly around me.

"Walter is the idiot—not you. You are a kind, thoughtful, amazing woman."

I shook my head. "I am not."

"You most certainly are." He kissed my forehead. "So is that when you moved back here? After you broke off the engagement?"

"Yes. Aunt Star suggested it, and it didn't take much convincing. The church secretary job opened up, and I jumped on it. The first few months I was here, several men asked me out on dates, but I turned them all down. I didn't trust myself to choose wisely anymore. I didn't want to fall back into my old habits."

"But then you met me, and I was irresistible," Mitchell teased.

"Pretty much." I smiled. "The first time you touched me—do you remember?"

"I'll never forget it. You got into Starla's car outside the bar, and I couldn't stop myself from putting my hand on your shoulder, just to see if it would be as electrifying as I hoped. It was."

"I felt that touch for *days.*"

Mitchell's laugh rippled through me.

I continued, "I hadn't felt that kind of instant attraction in ages. And while I was frustrated by all the obstacles thrown into our path over the months after we met, I was also grateful for them, because we were forced to take our relationship painfully slow. I didn't want to make the same mistake with you I'd made before. I wanted to make sure I didn't want to fix you."

"Baby, don't you know I'm perfect? Nothing needs fixing here."

I raised an eyebrow at him. "No?"

"Absolutely not." He tickled my side, and I squealed and swatted his hand away.

He continued, "So once circumstances didn't force us to take things slow any more, why did you still want to?"

"There's several reasons." I held up one finger. "First, I

still don't fully trust myself. I'm afraid I'll fall head over heels for you and *then* find out something about you that will make me slip into my old ways, and I'll be trapped."

"You're still afraid of that?"

"Maybe a little."

He gave me a squeeze. "I can't promise you'll never find out anything about me you won't like, but I do promise to tell you if I ever feel like you're trying to fix me."

"I have no doubt about that. And even if you didn't, Aunt Star would tell me."

"Starla's a peach."

"She is. The second reason I want to take things slow still stands—at least in one aspect of our relationship."

"I'm not sure I like where this is going."

"Just listen. This is something I've promised myself with each guy I've dated, and I stuck to it with everyone but Walter. He wasn't on the same page as me on it, and I didn't have the confidence and courage to stand up to him. This time I will follow through because it is extremely important to me." I took a deep breath and could feel my face flushing. "There are some things I'm not going to do with you before we're married."

NINE

MITCHELL'S SILENCE AND STILLNESS after my declaration made my heart stop. I twisted on his lap so I could see his face, which held an unreadable expression.

"You want to marry me?" he finally asked as a smile spread across his face.

My eyes opened more widely than I thought possible, and I clapped my hand over my mouth. Mitchell grasped my wrist and pressed my hand against his chest.

"Th-th-that's ...," I stuttered, "that's not what I was saying."

His heart pounded beneath my hand. "You said, 'before we're married,' which sounds like marriage is the conclusion you're seeing for us. Is it?"

My own heartbeat drummed in my ears. "Please don't ask me yet. I'm not at the point where I can take that step." I wasn't even sure I loved him yet. There was no way I was prepared to tell him I'd marry him someday.

"Can we talk about why?" I had never seen such an intense look in his eyes.

"In a minute. What about the other part of what I said— the thing I was really getting at?" I held my breath.

"If it's important to you, then it's important to me. I promise to help you keep your promise."

The air escaped my lungs in a *whoosh,* and I wrapped my arms around his neck. "Thank you."

"I'm glad I can still kiss you, though." As if to prove it, he caught my lips with his and we didn't talk about anything for a few minutes.

"Now let's talk about marriage," he said when we reluctantly pulled apart.

"Mitchell."

"Hypothetically."

We did need to talk about it. "Okay. Do you want to always be a traveling detective?"

"I love doing it. I enjoy the variety, the new people I get to meet, and—you'll appreciate this—helping police departments and communities during a tough time. But I don't know if I want to do it forever. Why?"

"Because—hypothetically—I don't want to be a part-time wife. I don't want my kids to have a part-time dad."

His eyebrows arched. "We're talking about kids now?"

"No!" Then I thought back to my conversation with Aunt Star in the car. "We probably should, though. Do you want kids?"

"Seven."

I sucked in a breath. "Excuse me?"

"Kidding. Unless you want seven. Then we'd have seven." He tucked a curl behind my ear. "Hypothetically."

"I do not want seven kids."

"Noted. But you want some?"

I nodded.

"Good," he said. "Me, too. As for my job, I ultimately don't care where it is or even what it is, as long as I enjoy it. I'm not committed to doing my current job forever. I do want to stay in law enforcement, though."

"What if you lived here in Cherry Hill?" I asked. "What

would your options be?"

"I've thought about it, and I don't think Darren and I could both work in the department full-time. The chief will be retiring soon, and Darren is his natural successor. Darren loves this town, and I can't imagine a better person to run the police department." He shrugged. "He already pretty much does anyway. I'm not going to try to come in and take the chief's job out from under him. He has more than earned it. But I also can't see it working out well with Darren as my boss. We get along fine with what we've done so far, but I don't think it would work long-term, especially with you and Starla thrown into the mix. Hypothetically speaking, of course."

"I get that, and I love that you've thought through not only what you want, but what's best for everyone. What about the County Sheriff's Department?"

"I am not a fan of Sheriff Stuckey."

"Neither am I. So if—*if*—someday in the distant future we were to decide to get married, that might mean living somewhere other than here?"

"Probably. Do you not want to leave?"

"Not really. I love being close to my parents and Aunt Star and Trixie. And I adore the church and the Cokers. I would leave if I really needed to, but I don't want to. It would be hard, especially when I have kids. I want a strong support system around me."

"Then I wouldn't want to make you leave." He leaned his head against mine.

"But I want you to have a job you love."

"We don't have to figure out our entire future right now. We can keep talking about this."

"We can," I said. "We will."

"Sure you don't want to promise right now that you'll marry me someday?"

I shook my head. "I already told you I can't do that yet."

"Okay. Do you have more reasons for taking things slow?" One corner of his mouth quirked up. "Or can we stop talking and do other things?"

I raised an eyebrow at him.

"I haven't forgotten our promise," he insisted. "I won't forget it. But there are plenty of things we *can* do."

I smiled at the prospect and was tempted to take him up on his offer, but I knew I needed to tell him everything about Marty. I couldn't put it off any longer.

Brrrrring!

"I should get that." I didn't move.

Brrrrring!

"Let the answering machine get it," Mitchell said.

Brrrrring!

I sighed. "Nobody calls at this time on a Sunday night without a very good reason."

Brrrrring!

I hurried to the kitchen and snatched up the phone before the answering machine kicked on.

"Beckett, it's Darren. Is Mitchell there?"

"Yes, why?"

"I need to talk to him."

"This can't wait until morning?"

"No, it's not about the case. Can you get him, please?"

I turned to call out for Mitchell, but he was standing in the kitchen doorway with his hands in his pockets. I held out the phone. "It's for you."

His brows furrowed, but he crossed the room and took the phone from me. The conversation was brief and consisted mostly of one-word responses on Mitchell's end. Partway through he turned away from me and his back muscles tensed. I slipped my hands around his waist from behind and pressed my cheek against his back, which slightly relaxed at my touch.

He hung up and turned in my arms, his face ashen.

"Mitchell! What's wrong?" I reached up and cupped his cheek.

"My friend Chris was in a car accident."

Mitchell had mentioned Chris many times. They'd been best friends their entire lives. Their parents were even best friends with each other. "Oh, I'm so sorry!" I pulled him closer and laid my head against his shoulder but then angled back to look at him. "Wait. How did Darren know about it?"

"My parents were trying to track me down and called the station. Darren told them he'd do his best to find me and let me know."

"Is he going to be okay?"

Mitchell gave me a confused look. "Who? Darren?"

I returned his confused look. "Noooo. Chris."

He closed his eyes and let out a long breath. When he opened his eyes again, his gaze was full of regret. "Chris is in critical condition—bad enough that I need to head to the hospital right now." He shut his eyes as he added, "And Chris isn't a 'he.'"

I took a step back, and our arms fell to our sides. "What are you saying?" I whispered, already knowing the answer.

"Chris is a woman." He opened his eyes but didn't look at me.

His words hit my chest like a fist. I gasped for breath, took a few more steps back, and grabbed onto the back of a kitchen chair before saying, "Your best friend is a woman, and you never thought to mention it?"

"Does it matter?"

"Mitchell, I don't care if your best friend is a ferret. What matters is you willfully hid that information from me, *and* you don't like me being friends with men, which seems to be extremely hypocritical right about now."

He looked at the floor and pressed his fingers to his temples. "I can't have this conversation now. I have to go."

"Then by all means, go," I said flatly. "But first, tell me one thing. Have you ever been more than friends with her?"

He avoided my gaze and didn't answer.

"Mitchell, look at me," I demanded.

He slowly moved his eyes to mine. They were full of pain—due to his answer to my question, his best friend being badly hurt, or both, I didn't know.

"I've kissed her." He looked away from me again. There was more he wasn't telling me.

I steeled myself. "Have you done more than kiss her?"

He slumped back against the kitchen counter, which unnerved me. Mitchell was always so confident and unflappable. He finally nodded.

"Did you like it?"

His gaze shot to mine, and his eyes flashed. "What kind of question is that?"

"The kind you'll answer if you care anything about me," I retorted.

"I care *so much* about you, Beckett." His voice broke when he said my name. "I love you."

Another invisible punch landed on my chest as rage threatened to fill me.

"No. Don't you dare say that right now."

"It's true."

"Yet you kiss and do who knows what else with your female best friend."

"Not anymore."

"Oh, that makes it better." I didn't even try to keep the sarcasm out of my tone. "Did you think I'd never find out? Did you honestly think you could potentially marry me, and I'd somehow never realize your best friend is a woman? Is that what you think of my mental ability?"

"Beckett, *please.*" His hands gripped the edge of the counter behind him so forcefully his knuckles turned white.

"Go." I pointed toward the door. "I can't look at you, and you have a *friend* to see." I regretted my statement as soon as I said it. I did care that he was hurting, though I was livid. As he passed by me, I grabbed his wrist. He stopped but didn't turn to me.

"I'm sorry for the way I said that. I hope she's okay. Truly."

He turned his head, focused his tortured gaze on me, and nodded. "I know you do." He twisted his wrist, and I let it drop.

I folded my arms in front of me as I silently watched him put on his coat and walk to the front door.

He turned to me as he opened it. "I'll call you in the morning?" His questioning tone told me he didn't assume I would want to talk to him, which I begrudgingly appreciated.

I pressed my lips together and nodded. If I said a word, I would burst into tears.

His free hand balled into a fist. "I'm sorry."
Then he was gone.

TEN

"HOW IS IT POSSIBLE that two men I care about told me they love me today, and I didn't want to hear it either time?"

Aunt Star stroked my hair as I lay on the couch with my head in her lap. "I don't know, honey."

My eyes were dry, and my body felt like it weighed a thousand pounds. I thought I would start sobbing the moment Mitchell disappeared through my door, but I didn't.

"I feel like such a hypocrite."

My aunt's hand stilled. "Why?"

"Because I didn't tell Mitchell everything about Marty either, did I?"

"It's not the same."

"It is. He kissed his female friend, and he didn't tell me. I almost kissed my male friend, and I didn't tell him."

"The 'almost' is the key word there. Plus, he admitted to doing more than kissing his friend. And you didn't try to hide the fact that Marty is a man and he wanted to date you. Mitchell was aware of both of those things. You also willingly chose to stay away from Marty because of your relationship with Mitchell. You're not in the wrong here, Becks."

"But I should have told him everything that happened with Marty a couple months ago."

"Okay, I'll give you that if you feel the need to beat

yourself up about something. But it's still not the same thing."

"He didn't trust me enough to tell me. That's what makes me so angry—and sad."

She turned my head so she could look me in the eye. "You didn't trust him enough to tell him everything either."

A lone tear trailed down my face, and Aunt Star wiped it away.

I said, "It's funny how we've kind of been together for nine months, yet there's so little we truly know about each other."

"The two of you have had an unconventional relationship, that's for sure. You might be right that the excitement of having to sneak around made you feel closer than you truly are. What do you think you want to do now?"

"I need to talk to him before I can fully figure out where to go from here. And I need to talk to Marty."

"Do you think Marty remembers what he said to you?"

"I have no idea. But either way, we need to talk. I can't leave his declaration hanging out there—especially not now."

"I think you're right. And I think we need to get to bed if we want to be worth anything at work tomorrow."

"I'm off through Wednesday, remember?" Tears filled my eyes. "Since Mitchell was supposed to be here with me during his vacation."

Aunt Star grabbed a tissue from the end table and handed it to me. "I'm sorry, Becks. I wish none of this was happening to you."

"Me, too."

———

BRRRRRING!

I groaned and rolled over in bed, wondering who was calling at such an ungodly hour.

Brrrrring!

Without opening my eyes, I determined to let my aunt pick it up from her room.

Brrrrring!

I opened one eye and realized my room wasn't completely dark. What time was it?

Brrrrring!

Finally, I reached over and grabbed the phone off my nightstand. "Hello?" I croaked.

"Beckett Lee Monahan, are you still in bed?"

"Good morning to you, too, Mom," I said groggily as I rubbed my eyes.

"Why aren't you up yet?" She paused. "Mitchell isn't there with you, is he?"

"Mom!"

"I'm only asking."

"Please don't ask me if there's a man in my bed ever again—even after I'm married. But anyway, he headed out last night."

"Oh."

"Oh, what?" I stretched and sat up in bed.

"I was going to see if the two of you wanted to meet your dad and me for lunch at the Dairy Queen." My parents were both taking off work at noon, as my brother's family would be arriving in the early afternoon. "Will Mitchell be back by then?"

"I don't know." I flopped back onto my pillow.

"You don't know."

"I do not."

"Care to tell me why?"

There was no reason not to tell her the bare facts. "Late last night he got a call that his best friend was in a car accident, and he needed to go to the hospital. I haven't heard from him yet this morning." I finally looked at the clock, which informed me it was almost 10:00. *Why hadn't he called?*

"Was it the accident with all those high school kids up near Jeff City?"

I lurched up again. "What are you talking about?"

"The drama club from a small school was in Jeff City last night to attend a Christmas performance, and their bus was hit by an eighteen-wheeler on their way home. On the morning news, they said the bus driver and one of the teachers were in critical condition, and a bunch of the kids were also in the hospital."

"What school?" I demanded. "What town?"

She said the name of Mitchell's hometown.

"Oh, no. I bet that's the accident she was in." I knew Chris was a teacher.

"She?"

I didn't mean to reveal Chris's gender, but there was no going back. "Mitchell's friend Chris."

"His best friend is a *woman?*"

I sighed. "Don't start, Mom."

"I don't like that idea one bit."

"It's none of your concern."

"It is if my daughter's boyfriend has a second girlfriend!"

My eyes widened. "Mom, can everyone at the bank hear you?" She was a teller at Cherry County Bank, and she often called me from the phone on the counter behind her window.

"I'm in the break room. The door isn't shut, but I doubt anyone heard me."

I groaned. "You practically shouted it."

"Even if they heard me, they won't know what I'm talking about."

"Mom, how many daughters do you have? And how many boyfriends do I have?"

"Just the one ... as far as I know."

"How would you not know if you have another daughter?" I wasn't going to touch the boyfriend question.

"You know what I meant."

"All right, Mom, I need to go. And you need to get back to work."

"Fine. Feel free to meet us at the DQ at noon if you're hungry."

"Thanks for the invitation. We'll see." There was no way I was going, as I had no desire to be interrogated about Mitchell.

As soon as I hung up the phone, it rang again.

"Hello?"

"Hi, Beckett."

Tingles ran up and down my spine at the sound of Marty's voice.

"Hi!" I said brightly. "How are you? Are you coming home today?"

"I'm feeling a little better. And I'm already home. They needed beds for some kids who were in a bus accident."

"Ah, I heard about that."

"Yeah, it was a terrible deal. Hey, as I was being wheeled out, I spotted Mitchell in the waiting room. Do you know why he was there?"

My chest tightened. "Yes, one of the teachers on the bus is a good friend of his."

"I'm sorry to hear that." He cleared his throat. "Listen, the reason I'm calling is because ... well, to talk about something I think I might have said to you on the phone yesterday."

So he did remember. "Um, yeah. We should talk, but not over the phone. Can I come over there, or will we have an audience?"

"I'm alone. Mom got me settled in and took off to do some Christmas prep, and Kyle's at work. Are you sure you want to do this in person?"

The conversation would be easier over the phone, but after my response to hearing his voice, I knew I needed to be in his presence to get a better idea of how I truly felt about him. "Yes, I'd prefer to come over."

"All right."

I couldn't go immediately, as I was still in my pajamas and my hair was undoubtedly out of control. "I'll be there in about forty-five minutes. Is that okay?"

"I'm not going anywhere. I'm supposed to take it easy the rest of the week. When you get here, knock and come on in."

———

MY EYES LOCKED ON Marty's the second I stepped into his living room, and my heart stopped when I spotted the white bandage encircling his head. Tears threatened to spill over, and my head spun. I stumbled to the end table near the door and leaned on it.

Alarm filled Marty's eyes, and he cranked down the feet of his recliner and was up and out of it before I could tell him to stay there. He stopped inches from me, his hands hovering at my shoulders. "I-I'm sorry," he said. "I don't know if I should ... are you okay?" The panic in his gaze didn't abate as we stared at each other.

I finally gave in and threw my arms around him. He wrapped me in a tight embrace, and a ripple of awareness spread throughout my body at his touch. He jerked away from me after a few seconds and my body swayed back toward his of its own accord, as if pulled by a magnetic force. My fingers itched to reach for him again.

"We can't do this." He attempted to run his fingers through his hair, but they got caught on his bandage. "This isn't right." He wobbled on his feet, and I grasped his arms to steady him.

"It's okay. Here, let me help you sit back down."

I guided him back to his seat and then sat in the chair across from him. As I tried to ignore the aftershocks running through my body, I avoided his eyes and looked around the room. My gaze stopped at the doorway into the kitchen.

"You haven't been here since that day, have you?" His voice was filled with compassion.

I didn't have to ask what day he meant—the one when a murderer held me at gunpoint in his kitchen. I shifted my focus to him and shook my head as tears filled my eyes again.

"Don't cry. Please." His hands clenched. "I don't think I can take it if you start crying and I can't comfort you."

I sniffled and wiped my eyes on my shirtsleeve. "I'll try not to."

"Can we get this over with?" His voice was laced with uncertainty, not frustration or impatience, as the question would typically imply.

"Yes. And I'm not going to make you repeat what you said. You were under the influence of some potent drugs." A corner of my mouth tipped up. "You were mostly hilarious, if I'm honest."

He briefly closed his eyes. "I don't remember everything I said, but I'm sure I don't want to be reminded of any of it." His eyes then laser focused on me. "I did mean what I told you, though. I shouldn't have said it, but since I did, you need to know I meant it." His gaze didn't waver. "I take those words—those feelings—very seriously. I've never said that to any other woman except my ex-wife."

My heart caught in my throat. I didn't know how to respond.

"I don't expect you to say it back or to even return those feelings," he said. "But can you say *something?* You did insist on coming over here to talk about this."

I nodded and bit down on my cheek to keep myself from crying. "I don't know exactly how I feel about you, Marty. But I do know I care for you a lot. And if it weren't for Mitchell ..." I wasn't sure I should finish that statement, or even how I would finish it.

"If it weren't for Mitchell, what?"

I shook my head. "When I touch you, I ... feel things." My face flushed. "Not friendly things."

"I know." His tone was confident but not cocky. "I can tell. I feel it, too."

"And I love talking to you. I miss that so much." I looked at the ceiling to keep tears from spilling out. "I wish I had gotten to know you before I met Mitchell." As soon as those words came out of my mouth, I realized what they meant. I cared for him at least as much as I did for Mitchell—maybe more. If I didn't, the sequence of events wouldn't matter.

A glimmer of hope filled Marty's eyes and he leaned forward slightly. "What are you saying?"

"I'm not saying I love you. But this isn't only friendship between us. I'm not naïve enough to think it is or even can be anymore." My connection with Marty was different than it was with Mitchell, but it wasn't any less real for not being as exciting. "Did you really think we could just be friends, the first time I talked to you yesterday?"

"No. I wasn't as drugged up then as I was later, but I wasn't completely in my right mind. I wouldn't have suggested it if I was."

I nodded.

"So what about Mitchell?" he asked.

"Things with Mitchell are ... well, I don't know."

"Does your sudden uncertainty about him have anything to do with the teacher in the hospital?"

I sat up straight. "Why would you say that?"

"Because the teacher who's in critical condition is a woman. It's not hard to put two and two together." His jaw clenched. "Is he dating her, too?"

"No." I twisted my hands together. "At least, I don't think so." I sighed. "I guess I'm not sure."

He groaned and closed his eyes. "Beckett, you're killing me. I want to punch that guy in the face for even letting you wonder for a minute if he has another girlfriend."

I gave him a tiny smile. "You'd never punch him, and you know it."

"Don't be so sure."

We were silent for a moment.

"I hope you don't mind me prying," I said, "but you

mentioned your ex-wife earlier, and I'm wondering why you got divorced."

"I don't mind. It's important for you to know, if there ever might be something between us. We rushed into marriage. We did love each other, but we didn't spend enough time— or really any time—talking about what we wanted long-term before we got married. We knew we both wanted to get married and have kids, and I guess we assumed we were on the same page about everything else."

He pulled at a loose string on the arm of his chair. "Turned out she dreamed of an exciting life. She wanted to move to the city, go on exotic vacations, and do fancy things all the time. I didn't. Ultimately, I probably would have given in and done it all, but she decided to find someone who wanted that same life without reservation. Most people think we simply fell out of love and decided to cut our losses, but she had an affair and left me for him. They got married a few months after our divorce was final."

"Marty, I'm so sorry."

He shrugged. "It is what it is. I would never have left her—I vowed before God that I would stand by her forever, and I was determined to keep my word—but we never would have been truly happy together. And now you know if you're looking for an exciting life somewhere away from Cherry Hill, I'm not the man to do that with. I'm not saying I would never go on vacations or do any of those other things, but I'm a simple man. That's not the kind of life I want all the time. I'd rather be here in Cherry Hill, near my family and friends, where everyone knows me and I know them."

Tears began trickling down my face as he finished speaking. "Me, too," I choked out. "I'd rather be here, too."

But Mitchell wouldn't, I added to myself.

Marty's hands flexed on the arms of his chair. "You said you wouldn't cry."

"I can't help it." I swiped my hands across my cheeks. "There's something you should know about me, too." I looked down at my lap. "I haven't been married before, but I've been engaged."

"I know."

My head snapped up. "You do?"

"Your mom loves to brag about you. Everyone knew you were engaged."

"My mom brags about me?" She rarely said anything positive about me in my presence.

"Whenever I go in the bank, she can't stop singing your praises."

"Oh." I had difficulty processing the information. I shook my head to refocus on our conversation. "You don't know this part of the story, though." I told him about Walter and how I'd always tried to fix the men I dated.

"So you're afraid you might try to do that again?" he asked when I was finished.

"Yes."

"You could be right." He held up a hand to stop my retort. "It's in your nature to help people. That's admirable. What's not admirable is when people take advantage of your desire to help and to fix things, which is what all those men did. I won't do that. You and I would be a team—helping each other through our problems. In fact, we've already done that. After all we both went through in the spring and summer, we helped each other deal with the fallout. Right?"

I nodded as my chest tightened and tears welled up yet

again.

"You didn't try to fix me," he continued. "I didn't try to fix you. We worked together to come out the other side of all that mess without lasting damage. We'll never be the same as we were before, but I'd say we're better for having walked through it together. Wouldn't you?"

"Yes," I said as I wiped my eyes.

"So where does all this leave *us?*" He motioned between us.

"I'm still dating Mitchell, as far as I know." Though I did wonder, as he hadn't called yet. "I need to talk to him before I make any decisions about any of this."

"I understand. But even if you don't keep dating him, I'm not going to ask you out for a couple months at least. I won't be your rebound. I want you to be one hundred percent sure of what you want before we start anything."

I nodded and stood. "I'll let myself out. And I'll talk to you again soon. I promise I won't leave you hanging."

ELEVEN

I OPENED THE FRONT door of Marty's house to leave, and I almost jumped out of my skin. A woman holding a Dutch oven stood on the front porch. She was one of the most stunning women I'd ever seen, and she was dressed to the nines, which was rather startling for a Monday morning in Cherry Hill.

"Hi," she said sunnily. "Are you Marty's sister?"

"Oh, no," reached my ears from across the room.

"I am not."

The woman frowned. "Then who are you?"

"Beckett Monahan. Who are you?"

Her eyes narrowed, and she didn't answer my question. "What are *you* doing here?"

The sound of the recliner's feet going down caught my attention, along with some muttering. I had a strong inclination the woman in front of me was Patty.

"I could ask you the same thing," I responded.

The woman stood up as straight as she could and said, "I'm bringing some soup to my boyfriend, thank you very much." She put a foot on the threshold, but I didn't move to let her in.

I put my hands on my hips. "He's not your boyfriend."

"Says who? You?" She laughed.

"No," Marty said from behind me, "says me." He gently

nudged me out of the way and faced Patty.

"Marty! You shouldn't be up. The doctor said—"

He interrupted her, "I don't know how you know what the doctor said, but that's nothing to do with you." He swayed slightly and braced himself against the doorframe. "Thank you for your concern, but you are not my girlfriend—not now, not ever. I'd like you to leave. I need to rest."

"Babe, you don't know what you're saying," she said soothingly. "The drugs must still be affecting you."

"The pain medication has worn off, and I won't be taking any more." He shot a glance at me. "I have complete control over what I'm saying."

"I don't think you do," she said, "but I can tell when I'm not wanted." She stooped and set the pot on the floor inside the door. "I'll be back tomorrow."

As she walked away, Marty called after her, "Please don't come back."

She simply flapped her hand at him and kept walking.

"Patty …"

I put a hand on his arm. "Let her go."

He shut the door and turned to me. "I haven't seen the last of her, have I?"

"No."

"How in the world does she know where I live?"

"Phone book, I'd guess. Let me help you back to your chair."

He protested, but he also staggered with his first step, so he allowed me to help. Then I took Patty's Dutch oven to his kitchen. He swore he wouldn't touch whatever was in it, but I couldn't leave it on the floor.

"Marty?" I stood at his front door, poised to leave.

"Yes?"

I knew I shouldn't go on this fishing expedition, but I couldn't stop myself. "Are you sure you don't want to see Patty again?"

"Positive. Why?"

"She's gorgeous."

"And pushy and annoying and stalkery." I noted he didn't deny she was beautiful.

"Stalkery?" I teased.

He snorted. "Definitely stalkery."

"A little drugged-up birdie also told me she's a terrible kisser." I pressed my lips together so I wouldn't laugh.

Marty covered his face with his hands. "I did say that, didn't I?"

"You did."

"Well, it's true." He put his hands down and his tone turned serious. "But even if she wasn't any of those things I just mentioned, I wouldn't want to date her."

Again, I knew I shouldn't ask, but I did, even though I was pretty sure I knew the answer. "Why?"

"Because she's not you."

We locked eyes for several seconds before I exited without another word.

———

"Hi, Barbara. Is Darren here?" I asked the receptionist at the police station.

"Yes, let me see if he's free." She bustled into the pit, leaving me standing in the lobby.

When I passed the police station on my way home from

Marty's house, I realized I never got the details of what happened with the robberies. Mitchell's truck wasn't in the parking lot, so I decided to stop and talk to Darren.

"You can go on back," Barbara said as she returned.

Several heads turned toward me as I walked through the pit, and one officer grinned at me. I smiled back before I realized why he was grinning. How had it not even been twenty-four hours since Mitchell kissed me in the chief's office with the entire building watching? My face turned red as I approached Darren's office.

"Everything okay?" he asked as I entered and closed the door behind me.

"Yes."

He didn't believe me, but he didn't push it. "What do you need?"

"I was wondering where the case stands."

"Mitchell didn't tell you?"

"We didn't get a chance to talk about it before he left last night. And I haven't talked to him yet today."

"Oh." He gave me a shrewd look but didn't say what he was thinking.

"Well, what can you tell me?"

"The kids were hanging out at one of their houses and drinking. I think a couple of them were smoking pot, too, but they wouldn't admit to it. One of them dared the others to break into a house, and they were dumb enough and drunk enough to do it. When they were successful at Suzanne's, they got smug and tried again at your house." He nodded toward me. "You and Mitchell were right about scaring them off. Why that didn't put an end to it, I don't know, but instead they decided they could find some good stuff at the hardware store. The kid who hit Marty feels terrible about it. I'm pretty sure he was both drunk and high at the time."

"What was the deal with the last kid, who we saw out at the barn?" I asked.

"He's not technically a kid. He's older than the others—twenty-two. And he was the ringleader. He knew we were catching up with everyone else, and he was scared. He was afraid we'd track the stuff to Celia's dad's house, since we'd taken her in, so he was trying to move it all out to the barn on his grandparents' property. He had only taken one small load out before we got to the house."

"What will happen to them?" I asked.

"That's up to the judge," Darren explained. "Ted Posey is probably looking at a stint in juvie. The twenty-two-year-old will likely spend some time in jail. The rest of them should get off a little easier, since they're minors, weren't armed, and confessed. But there will be consequences for all of them."

"I feel bad for them," I said.

"Don't. They need to learn their lesson before they do something even dumber."

I nodded. "What's going to happen with our Christmas gifts?"

"You'll get most of them back later today. Starla came in earlier and went through it all with me, so you don't need to worry about dealing with any of that." He crossed his arms. "You're not going to tell me what happened with Mitchell?"

"Why do you think something happened? Did Aunt Star say something to you?"

"No. She wouldn't. I'm asking because you're not your usual happy self and because I haven't heard from him today, either."

I hung my head. "I can't tell you what happened. It wouldn't be right, since you work with him. Plus, I don't fully know what's going on myself."

"Let me know if I need to have a little chat with him."

I appreciated his protectiveness, but I couldn't get him involved. "I'll be fine."

"But if you're not, you know you can always come to me, right?"

"I know. And I love you for it."

———

"BECKETT, WE NEED TO TALK. Please call me at this number as soon as you can." Mitchell's voice rattled off a number. I rewound the tape on the answering machine to play it back so I could write it down. Then I sat staring at it while sitting at the kitchen table. I was still there when the overhead garage door screeched open several minutes later. I looked at the clock and was surprised to note it was past noon.

Aunt Star momentarily stopped in the doorway from the garage when she saw my face. Then she strode swiftly in my direction and put her arms around my shoulders from behind. "I love you, Becks." She gave me a squeeze and then sat across from me. I reached my hand out, and she took it in hers.

"Mitchell wants to talk." I tapped the phone number with my free hand.

"Are you ready to talk to him?"

"No, but I won't be any more ready an hour from now."

"Then get it over with. You need to do it before your brother's family gets here, anyway. You know you want to see the kids the second they arrive at your parents' house. I'll go upstairs and give you some privacy."

"No, I'll call him from my room." I pushed myself up from the table. Before I headed upstairs, I said, "I saw Marty."

Her eyebrows shot up. "You did? He's home?"

"Yes."

"How did that go?"

"I'll tell you after I talk to Mitchell."

"Okay. Go. Have you eaten lunch?"

"No. I haven't eaten anything all day. I don't feel like it."

"You need to eat something. I'll run to The Check and pick up a few things while you're on the phone."

I settled myself on my bed with a box of tissues, took a few deep breaths, said a quick prayer, and dialed the phone. A hospital receptionist answered.

"Um, hello, I'm trying to get in touch with Mitchell Crowe."

"Yes," she said. "Is this Beckett?"

My eyebrows drew together. "It is."

"Are you at home?"

"Yes." Why did she need to know where I was?

"He said to tell you he'll call you right back."

"Oookay. Bye, then."

The dial tone buzzed, and I stared at the phone before hanging it up. A few minutes later it rang. Out of pettiness, I let it ring three times before answering it.

"Hello?" I said as a question, as if I didn't know who was calling.

"Hi." Even with that one syllable, Mitchell's voice was guarded.

"How's Chris?"

"You really want to know?"

His surprise irked me.

"Of course I do. I'm not a monster."

"I know you're not. She's not doing great, but they're almost certain she'll pull through."

"I'm so relieved to hear that."

"Me, too." He took a deep enough breath I could hear it. "I'm sorry about what happened last night."

"Which part?"

"Everything after Darren called, I guess."

"Mmhm." If he wasn't going to get into specifics, I wasn't going to engage in the conversation.

After a few seconds, he said, "I should have told you about Chris."

"What should you have told me?"

"First, that she's a woman. Second, that we dated for a while."

"A while? How long is 'a while'?"

He sighed, which was annoying. He didn't get to sigh in this situation.

"As you know," he said, "we've been friends our entire lives. A few years back, we were both single and decided we'd try dating. It didn't work out in the end, but we were able to stay friends afterward."

"How long is 'a while'?" I repeated.

He hesitated. "Nine months, give or take."

"Nine months is a little longer than 'a while' in my book. How long ago was this?"

"About a year and a half ago."

"You started dating a year and a half ago, or you stopped

dating then?"

He sighed again. "Started."

I quickly did the math in my head. "Were you still dating her when you met me?" I asked between clenched teeth.

"No, we broke up a couple weeks before."

Was I his rebound? I didn't like the feeling I might be. And I didn't like how he was trying to avoid fully answering my questions.

"Can you forgive me?" he asked.

"For what?"

"You're not going to make this easy for me, are you?"

He sounded defeated, but I didn't give in. "No."

"Will you forgive me for being an idiot and not telling you any of this a long time ago?"

How could I not forgive him, when I hadn't told him everything, either? "I forgive you, but that doesn't mean we're okay. You should have told me, and you haven't mentioned anything about your double standard of having a female best friend *who you recently dated* when you don't like me being friends with Jeff or Marty—one of whom I dated ten years ago in high school, and the other whom I've never dated."

"I'm sorry about that, too."

"Okay." Though I no longer wanted to tell him what happened with Marty a few months earlier, I wouldn't forgive myself if I didn't admit I had held that back from him, too. "I have something to admit on the Marty front."

"Oh?"

"I almost kissed him back in October."

"You what?!" he shouted.

"I don't think you get the right to be angry about that."

"I think I do. I didn't kiss Chris while I was dating you!"

"And I didn't kiss Marty."

"But you wanted to?"

"I didn't not want to," I hedged. I wasn't going to give him the details.

"I cannot believe this."

"Mitchell, I cut him out of my life for you."

"I didn't ask you to do that."

"I know, but you wanted me to. Deny it if it's not true."

He was silent.

"Exactly." I punched my pointer finger into my mattress for emphasis.

"Where do we go from here?" he asked after a time of awkward silence.

"How do you feel about Chris? Do you love her?"

"She's my best friend. Of course I love her," he said.

"That's not what I'm asking. How did you feel when you heard about her accident?"

He hesitated. "I don't think you want to know."

"I'm certain I want to know the truth—the whole truth."

He was silent for a few moments before he said with emotion, "I felt like my heart was being ripped out of my chest."

Surprisingly, I didn't have the same feeling in response to his declaration. "I think you love her as more than a friend."

"I love *you,*" he replied.

"You don't."

"I do."

"Maybe so. But you love her, too." I wrapped the phone cord around my finger and watched the tip turn purple while I waited for him to respond.

"No. I can't love two women at the same time."

"You can." I unwound the cord, amazed at how calm I was. "It's entirely possible. But you can't be with both of us. And I'm going to make the decision easy for you."

"No. Don't do this," he warned.

"You and I are going to take a break. We won't see each other or even talk to each other for two months. When that time is up, we'll both see where we stand."

"Do I get any say in this plan?"

"You can get on board with my proposition, or we can completely end things right here and now. And before you think I'm being either selfless or spiteful, you need to know I'll be spending those two months evaluating not only my feelings for you but also for Marty."

"Are you *kidding* me?"

"Seriously, Mitchell, listen to yourself." I shook my head. "You have no room to talk."

He sighed again. "I guess we'll do it your way, then."

"You're not helping your cause right now, you know."

"You really need to cut me some slack here. I've slept about two hours since Saturday morning."

My heart softened toward him a bit. "You're right. I'm sorry. I'll let you go. And I'm really glad Chris is going to be okay."

"Thank you for saying that. I'm truly sorry, baby. I'm sorry I didn't trust you enough to be completely honest with you. Please believe me."

"I do believe you. And I'm sorry I didn't trust you enough to tell you everything, either."

"I don't want to hang up. I don't want this to be over."

I couldn't say the same. I felt oddly free. "I'll talk to you in two months. Now go get some sleep."

TWELVE

"YOU REALLY FEEL OKAY about everything with these guys?" Aunt Star asked.

"I do," I said from across the table as we ate our lunch. "I'm sad about Mitchell, but I'm not devastated. It's strange. Last night he and I were talking about the potential of marriage, and now we're taking a break and I'm considering possibly dating someone else. What does that say about me? Am I that fickle?"

"No. You had very good reasons to put things on hold with him, even without the Marty factor. There will be moments over the next couple months when you'll wonder if you made the right decision today." She waved her sandwich at me. "But that's why this break is a good idea. You need time to figure out if you want to date either one of them. And you need to think about it that way. This isn't necessarily about choosing between the two of them. It's about figuring out what you want for your future and then determining whether either of them might fit into it."

———

"HELLO?"

I was pretty sure the woman answering Marty's phone wasn't Patty, but I couldn't be certain based on one word.

"Is Marty there?" I asked.

"Yes, can I tell him who's calling?"

"Beckett Monahan." I braced myself for the woman's response.

"Oh, hi, Becky. This is Marty's mom."

My body relaxed. "Hi, Mrs. James." I was acquainted with his mom but didn't know her well.

"Please call me Sharon."

"Okay, Sharon."

"Marty's in bed, but I just left him, so I don't think he's asleep. Hold on."

I heard a click, some mumbling and scuffling, and another click.

"Hey there." Marty's voice sent warmth flowing through me.

"You doing okay?"

"I'm trying to get comfortable in my bed. My head throbs when it's not elevated, but I'm not feeling too terrible."

I blurted out, "I talked to Mitchell." There was no reason to beat around the bush.

"And how did that go?" he asked in a pleasant tone. I knew him well enough to know he was faking it.

"I won't give you the details, but we're taking a break."

"Oh?"

"Yes. For two months. We're not going to see each other or even talk. I need to figure out how I feel about him and what I want for my future." I took a deep breath. "And I need to figure out how I feel about someone else."

"I really hope you're talking about me and not yet another man."

I chuckled. "Yes, it's you. I know we've already gone two

months without talking, but I need another two. I assume you'll be fine with that, based on what you said earlier."

"Yes. I don't love the idea, but it's for the best."

"It is."

"Does anyone else know about this? About what I said to you and this whole two-month thing?"

"Aunt Star knows. She was sitting right next to me during the infamous phone call. And I tell her almost everything anyway. But she won't tell a soul. I'll also tell Trixie … unless you don't want me to."

"Please tell her. I want you to be able to talk to your friends about something this important—especially friends who like me." I could hear the grin in his voice.

I laughed. "I'll likely also talk to Veronica about you, but nobody else. Your secret will be safe with us."

"I hope someday it's not a secret."

We were both silent for a while. I didn't want to hang up, and I was sure he didn't either.

"I miss you already," he finally said.

"Yeah," I whispered. "I miss you, too."

THE NEXT AFTERNOON, our living room was once again strewn with torn wrapping paper, but the mood was quite different than on Saturday night. The tree lights twinkled, Alabama's new Christmas album played in the background, and everyone was content—even me.

Rafe and Cari were trying to teach Brandon how to use his Teddy Ruxpin, but he kept getting distracted by his G.I. Joe figures. Jodie was changing the clothes on her Cabbage

Patch Doll for the fifteenth time, and she had roped Aunt Star into helping her. Darren and Dad were attempting to hook the Nintendo up to the TV while I read the instructions to them, which they completely ignored. Mom was nowhere to be seen—probably in the kitchen, against my commands.

Aunt Star caught my eye and smiled. She gave me an "are you okay" look. I nodded and then touched my throat while raising an eyebrow at her. She lifted a hand and stroked her new diamond necklace. Darren honored her wish not to give her a ring, but he still managed to give her a diamond. She seemed happy with it.

Jodie skipped over to me. "Do you like the watch I picked out for you, Aunt Beck?" She tapped the colorful Swatch on my wrist.

"I love it so much! And I love *you* so much!" I pulled her into a hug and then tickled her. She shrieked and collapsed into giggles on my lap.

"I like your fingernails," she said as she stroked my red and green nails.

"You want me to paint yours later?"

"Yes!"

"Ask your mom if it's okay."

"It's fine." Cari smiled at us from across the room. "You know she wants to be you when she grows up, right?"

I hugged my niece again. "You sure you want to be me and not somebody famous like Alyssa Milano or Whitney Houston or Princess Leia?"

Jodie pursed her lips. "Princess Leia isn't real."

"I know, but she's pretty cool."

"She is, but she's not *you.* You're my favoritest favorite, Aunt Beck!" She threw her arms around my neck.

I wrapped my arms around her little body again and held her tightly until she wriggled free. She started to walk away but then came back and put her lips to my ear.

"I have a secret," she whispered. "It's super exciting!"

"What is it?" I whispered back.

"I can't tell you. Then it wouldn't be a secret, would it?"

"I won't tell anybody. I promise."

"I believe you. But I promised *I* wouldn't tell, so I can't."

"You're right," I said solemnly. "I don't want you to break your promise."

Ding-dong!

Aunt Star and I both automatically got up to answer the door, though I couldn't imagine who would be visiting on Christmas Eve. I opened the door to reveal Celia Hunt standing on the sidewalk with her grandpa. At least, I assumed it was Celia. She stared at the ground with her hair falling in front of her face. Aunt Star and I both stepped outside the storm door onto the porch, and I wrapped my arms around myself to ward off the winter chill.

"Go on, Celia." Mr. Hunt gave her a nudge.

She peeked up through her hair. "I'm sorry for what I did."

I wanted to hug her, but her body language told me she wouldn't appreciate the gesture.

"I forgive you," I said.

Aunt Star hesitated, but she also accepted the apology.

"I'm glad you can be with your family for Christmas," I said to Celia.

"Yeah, me, too," she said with a small smile.

"We don't know yet what the full consequences of her actions will be," her grandpa said, "but I hope she has learned her lesson."

"I have," she said softly.

"Good," Aunt Star said. "Thanks for coming by. We'll let you get back home now." She put her hand on the storm door handle.

"We have two more stops to make before we can head back home," Mr. Hunt said grimly.

I descended the porch steps and put a hand on Celia's arm, and she stiffened for a moment before relaxing under my touch.

"I'd love to see you at church again, Celia," I said. "We have youth group every Wednesday night. You're welcome anytime."

She looked me fully in the eyes. "Thank you."

"I'll make sure she's there," her grandpa said. "Well, unless she's away for a while."

"Only come if you want to," I insisted to Celia. "I'm always there with Pastor Greg. We really would love to have you."

She nodded. Her grandpa thanked us for our time, and they left.

"That was interesting," my aunt said as we headed back inside.

"Indeed. Celia seems to be truly sorry."

"Maybe so. I can't imagine Suzanne will be as gracious as you were." She paused as we stood inside the front door. "I'll admit I wasn't feeling especially gracious myself."

"I think she just needs some people who care about her. Her grandparents don't seem like the most caring people in the world, though I'm sure they love her in their way. I hope she'll come to youth group."

Aunt Star put an arm around me. "If anyone can make her

feel like she belongs there, it's you. Now, let's get back to celebrating."

She rejoined Jodie on the floor, and I wandered into the kitchen in search of my mom. She was standing at the sink, staring out the window at the backyard.

"Mom, you okay?"

She turned to me with a dish in her hand, dripping soapy water onto the floor.

"You're not supposed to be doing the dishes!"

"You know me. I can't stand having dirty dishes sitting around." She looked down. "Whoops! I need to wipe that up before someone slips on it."

"Let me do it. And you put that dish down and go play with your grandkids."

I grabbed a towel and wiped up the soapy water from the floor.

"I'll be in there soon." She rinsed the dish and placed it in the drying rack. "Are you all right, honey?"

I paused before answering, mostly out of shock. She never called me "honey."

"I'm fine," I finally said.

"You sure? I was surprised when you said Mitchell wouldn't be here."

"We're taking a break." She would find out soon enough, so I figured I might as well tell her.

"Oh." She narrowed her eyes. "Is it because of that other woman?"

"There are several reasons for it that I don't want to get into." I pulled a dish out of the drying rack and wiped it with a fresh towel.

"You know you can talk to me about it if you need to,

right?"

"I know, Mom. But I'll be okay."

"All right." She handed me another dish to dry. "I like Mitchell, but lately I've been thinking he's not quite right for you."

That was news to me. "Why?"

"I couldn't quite put my finger on it, which is why I never said anything. But I was also afraid he would take you away from us."

"You don't want me to move away?"

"Of course not. I hated it when you were in St. Louis. And you know I can't stand the fact that your brother and the kids are all the way in Chicago."

"What are you saying about Chicago?" my brother asked as he entered the kitchen and headed toward us.

"I was saying I hate that you live so far away," Mom explained.

He leaned down and kissed her cheek. "Then you'll be happy to hear I'm transferring to the St. Louis office."

I knew Rafe's financial services firm had an office in Missouri, but I had no idea he was thinking of moving.

Mom dropped a plate into the sink and spun toward him, flinging soapy water across the front of his sweater in the process.

He held his arms out wide. "Merry Christmas!"

I beamed at my brother as Mom threw her arms around him and jumped up and down in a shocking display of emotion.

"My baby's coming home," she gushed. "I'm so happy."

"Mom, you're soaking me."

She stepped away from him and then swatted his arm.

"Why didn't you tell us sooner?"

I was surprised the kids hadn't given it away. The news was undoubtedly the secret Jodie was talking about.

"Well, I didn't find out for sure until last Friday. And I didn't want to make Christmas about me. It should be about all of us."

"But this *is* about all of us! You four are going to be so much closer to us. Why would we not want to celebrate that?"

My brother blushed. "You know I don't like being the center of attention. I'd rather tell people big news one at a time—not in a big group."

"Well, if you don't tell your dad and aunt right now, I'm going to tell them."

Keeping secrets was not in my mom's repertoire, which was one of the reasons she would not be finding out the details of what happened with Mitchell or Marty.

Rafe sighed. He knew there was no stopping her from carrying out her threat. "Let's go tell them, then."

I looped my arm through his as we headed back to the living room. "I'm glad you're coming back home—or at least closer to home."

"Me, too, Beck. Me, too."

If you enjoyed this book, join author D.A. Wilkerson's exclusive mailing list!

When you join the list, you don't just receive an email a few times a month. You get book and playlist recommendations, 1980s throwbacks, writing updates, sneak peeks of upcoming books, the potential of joining an upcoming book launch team, and much more. Come join the fun!

To join, go to danawilkerson.com and click "Sign Up."

Mystery Journals

Do you want an easy way to keep track of all the suspects or other characters in mysteries? These journals allow mystery readers to record suspects, other characters, motives, means, opportunity, and more!

Available at Amazon.com

Totally 80s Mysteries
Book 1

The year is 1985, and 28-year-old Beckett Monahan's job as a church secretary in her small hometown of Cherry Hill isn't glamorous, but it's about to get more exciting. When she stumbles onto a dead body at a wedding, she quickly involves herself in the investigation in order to clear the names of friends and loved ones.

While investigating, Beckett must deal with the reality that someone in Cherry Hill is a killer. She is also forced to hide her efforts from the local police, who have told her not to interfere. With the assistance of family members and friends, Beckett uncovers clues, debates suspects' motives, and makes clandestine outings to confirm her suspicions. Can she find the killer before they take her out of the picture?

Available at your favorite online bookseller.

Totally 80s Mysteries
Book 2

The Class of 1975 is back in Cherry Hill for their ten-year reunion, and they're in for a totally wild surprise. When a classmate is murdered, Beckett is determined to track down the killer, who is almost certainly one of her childhood friends. She knows who was most popular and most likely to succeed, but which of her former classmates is most likely to kill?

Complicating matters, Detective Mitchell Crowe is back on the scene as Beckett's reunion date. However, as he takes the lead in the investigation, their budding relationship is put on hold again. Will this latest roadblock draw the two of them together or push them apart?

Available at your favorite online bookseller.

Totally 80s Mysteries
Book 3

1985 has not been kind to the small town of Cherry Hill. After two murders, the citizens want nothing more than a peaceful fall. Imagine their dismay when a local bank is robbed and a man's life hangs by a thread. Once again, church secretary Beckett Monahan vows to find the culprits.

As if solving an armed robbery isn't enough, Beckett also must cope with suddenly becoming the most popular single woman in town. It seems every unmarried man she knows carries a torch for her. All Beckett wants is to date Detective Mitchell Crowe after months of waiting, but the men of Cherry Hill seem to have other plans for her.

Will Beckett be able to focus on the case while dealing with all the men in her life? Can she finally solve a crime without getting herself into a life-or-death situation? Find out in *Of Heist and Men!*

Available at Amazon.com.

FIND
D.A. Wilkerson online!

Instagram
@d.a.wilkerson.author

Facebook
@dawilkersonauthor

Tiktok
@dawilkersonauthor

Website
danawilkerson.com

About the Author

D.A. (Dana) Wilkerson is the author of the Totally 80s Mysteries cozy mystery series. She has been a professional writer and editor for almost two decades and was the collaborative writer of two non-fiction *New York Times* best sellers: *The Vow: The True Events That Inspired the Movie* (Kim and Krickitt Carpenter) and *Balancing It All* (Candace Cameron Bure).

Dana lives in Oklahoma and enjoys traveling, reading, being an aunt, binge-watching crime shows, and attending Oklahoma City Thunder basketball games.

Made in United States
North Haven, CT
24 December 2023

46568744R00086